Aliferous

A collection of
Fairy Tales, Adventure, Romance & Whimsy

Aliferous

A collection of
Fairy Tales, Adventure, Romance & Whimsy

ALISSA J. ZAVALIANOS

All bird facts taken from Google or the Cornell Lab of Ornithology.

Printed in the United States of America

Edited by Micaiah Keough
Proofread by Caitlin Miller
Cover design by Alissa J. Zavalianos
Graphics & Images from Canva

ISBN 979-8-9881439-3-2 (paperback)
ISBN 979-8-9881439-2-5 (hardcover)
ISBN 979-8-9881439-4-9 (ebook)

To my nieces and nephews—Brody, Bentley, Kaleb, Kayra, Mia, and Amira—who fill my life with such joy. I hope these stories remind you that it's okay to grow up, but you can always remain a child at heart.

And to the little one who made me a mom—we love you already. Mommy and Daddy can't wait to meet you this spring.

Table of Contents

Endings & Things

Dear Reader,

Before you embark on this adventure, let me tell you a little more about this collection and why I decided to write it. *Aliferous* is a fifteen years-long endeavor with stories written in my teens, early twenties, and on the cusp of turning thirty. In many ways, these stories have grown me and grown with me; they're a culmination of my childhood musings meeting my nostalgia and wonder as an adult, particularly revolving around birds and the beauty of God's creation.

And now I get to share them with you.

My hope is that these tales and poems remind you it's never a wrong time to dream, and growing up is but another grand adventure. Wonder abounds around every corner if only we would open our eyes enough to look for it.

So pull up a chair, grab a warm cuppa, and let's dive in together.

> "Outside in a wooded glen
> Beneath the creaking boughs,
> Magic stirs the air—
>
> A call of the wren,
> A whisper of the wind,
> An invitation to draw near.
>
> To take up my pen
> Like the seeds in my hand
> And spend a while there."

With love,

Alissa

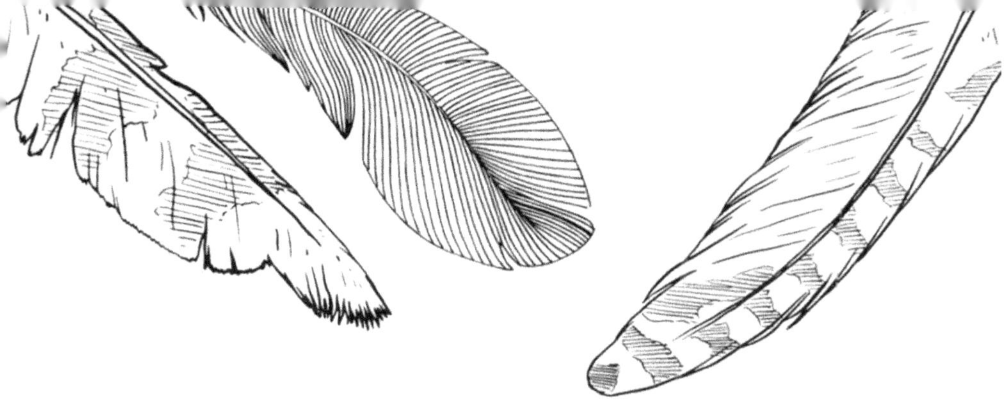

Fairy Tales

Anna Belle and the Seed

(A *Beauty and the Beast* inspired tale)

"Some humility can thaw even the coldest of hearts and cause things to grow in the foulest of weather."

Part One

My Predicament

It's been three days, and we still have no idea where she could be!" my mother says. I see her pacing the kitchen when I look up through the large window stationed above the sink.

My father sits at the kitchen counter, and I imagine the coolness of the marble countertop chilling the fabric beneath his elbows. They exchange glances. Mother wipes her powdered face, and I know she's crying even though I can't see the tears. Their voices continue to filter through the slight crack in the window and into the chilly morning, the crisp air carrying their words to my ears.

"I know, Jen. I'm going to hang up more posters before I head to work and make a few more calls to the police. We'll find her. I don't think I can take those photographers any longer, standing outside our house and trying to get information." My father stands up and walks to the front window and peaks outside. The way his back stiffens makes me question what he sees. He turns to face my mother, his mouth agape.

"Honey, promise me things will be okay," she pleads.

Father walks back over to the table and puts on his tailored jacket and the suede scarf one of my sisters gave him for Christmas. "Things will be okay." He kisses her and rounds the mahogany staircase that leads to the four-car garage.

The imported Prius he bought me for my eighteenth birthday is in there, and I remember how I refused to drive it because I had wanted a Mini Cooper convertible instead. The memory has my conscience bristling.

My parents told me I was ungrateful, but at the time, I just thought they failed to meet my expectations. *They care more about the environment than they do for me.* But I got over it once I held the coveted iPod they'd been loath to give me.

Not like it would do me much good *now*, considering…

The sound of a car's humming engine starting up distracts me from my thoughts. As it slowly fades away, I see the retreating form of a black Highlander Hybrid exit Fairfield Estates, chased by a mob of hungry flash photography. *Who knew being a lawyer could warrant so much unwanted publicity? Especially when one's daughter is missing.*

I return my gaze to the window and see that my mother has taken a seat at the kitchen table, her head in her hands, shoulders shuddering with sobs. I feel compelled to comfort her, but there's little use that'd do, seeing as I'm no longer a friend of doorknobs. Besides, I'm too busy trying to get this stupid seed to sprout. I've been sitting here all day, my underside like some sort of incubator, but it's not budging in this frigid weather.

A lamb's bleat catches my attention, and I look up to see one steadily approach me. I try to ignore it, but its towering form keeps getting closer.

I never liked going outside to feed the livestock—they were always dirty and smelly. *I should know.* But my parents *had* to buy a house with the largest plot of land so we could have our own farm, thinking it would prove a constructive and healthy outlet for me and my sisters. We had grown up rich, money on our metaphorical trees, but ever since my parents were humbled by the crash of the stock market and countless bouts of food poisoning, they became health freaks, "downsized," and moved here. Though some might say our elaborate décor and large house could still be classified as a mansion.

And for some reason, my sisters bought into it—shoveling cow dung, shearing the sheep, retrieving eggs from the unfortunate chickens. I wasn't so quick to warm up to the idea. Since moving, we had to let our maid and landscaper go. It stinks because now we all have to pull our own weight around here. Which is normal, sure—for *other* people. I never thought it'd be normal for *me.*

I'd rather do other things; I always wanted to become a computer engineer, but according to my parents, the "technological path is the world's greatest downfall." Hence why my mother is now a farmer and my father is a lawyer for families, not companies. I guess I'm not cut from the same cloth; I simply cannot win.

On one occasion, my mother came into my room and raised her voice. "Anna Belle Johnson, why do you have to be so selfish? Your sisters are working tirelessly on their chores while you just sit here on your computer!"

But I wasn't just *sitting*; I was fighting a cyber war. I was trying to combat the latest computer virus, so I never understood what was the big deal. Wasn't I still doing something helpful? And if not for my family, at least for all of humanity?

Besides, my annoying sisters were better suited for the job since they had no aspirations of their own—and still don't, might I add. Plus, there was nothing a few dollar bills couldn't fix.

I was doing something much more productive with my time.

So I sat there at my computer, blasted my music, and pretended I never heard a word. I had dreams, too, and I'd achieve them, whether or not my parents approved. Who cared what they said? They sure didn't care about me.

And seeing as things currently stand, it looks like they never will get the chance.

***

Hours pass, the sun begins its descent, and the seed still hasn't sprouted. My heart constricts inside my chest; is there any hope for me?

I gasp as my mother opens the back door and looks outside. She only ever comes out here to tend to the garden and the livestock, grabbing vegetables or one of the cured meats hanging in our meat shed out back. But it's the middle of winter, and there are no vegetables to be had. Besides, we ran out of cow meat last week.

Despite the local farmers markets nearby, my parents pride themselves on their newfound passion for growing fresh produce and cultivating livestock. The idea of pesticides and GMOs is too much for them to handle (and they think I'm high maintenance?).

But now, as she steps onto the frozen grass and closes the door behind her, my heart beats faster. I know I have to scurry away, and quickly, because she is headed right for me.

I dart beneath the chicken wire and shimmy under the coop as far as my small body will allow, but that does little to preserve my safety.

"Come here, darling," she coaxes, *cooing* of all things.

Despite my best efforts, two soft hands reach out and encircle my body, pulling me skyward. I hear the Leghorns, Buffs, and Wyandottes squawking their signals of victory by evading capture; they stare at me with their beady eyes as they emerge from under the coop and strut as if nothing happened at all. Some friends they are.

"We could all use something fresh for dinner," she continues, stroking my feathered head.

My feet kick back and forth, and I struggle like my life depends on it. But it hardly matters. I'm held captive in the arms of my mother.

Part Two

Before Something Fowl

It happened three days ago.

I was forced to go outside and take over Alice's chores. Apparently, my sister got pneumonia for leaving the house with wet hair; how tragic—more for me than her. At least she got to stay inside where it was warm. It didn't matter that she looked as if she received a kiss from death itself.

Alice, the youngest and most imaginative of my sisters, was always in her own little wonderland. She usually spread the chicken feed around the inside of the coop in the shape of different farm animals, which I thought took too much time. The blasted birds would trample all over it anyway. At least Margaret was sensible enough to simply fill the feeder and leave them be.

I, on the other hand, chucked the rubbish at the feathered creatures and threw out curses when they jabbed at my ankles.

"Filthy vermin! You can die for all I care! It'd be better for me so I wouldn't have to be out here with all of you!"

I was about to dump the last of the food on the fattest chicken when something grabbed my wrist and spun me in the opposite direction. It was a woman with eyes as deep and dark as pitch, wearing a hooded cloak that just barely covered her ankles. On her free arm rested a basket filled with seeds of all kinds, her long fingernails methodically tapping against their paper packaging.

"Get off me, old hag! Who are you?" I tried wrenching my wrist free from her grasp, but she only dug her nails deeper.

"Dearie, I'm someone you don't want to mess with." Her lips quirked into an unnerving smile.

"What are you doing here?" I narrowed my eyes.

"It's the principle of nature. You tend to things you want to grow."

"What does that even mean?"

"I've been watching you over the years, and tsk, tsk, tsk, you're a sad sight. You don't care for much other than yourself. You don't care about your sisters, your parents, nor these chickens. You want nothing to grow except your own selfish heart." She let go of my wrist to fish around in her basket amongst the bags of seeds.

"That's not true! They don't care about *me* and what *I* want! You left that part out," I retaliated, stomping my foot on the hard earth.

"And a nasty temper, too." The old woman finally found her desired packet. She opened it up and hobbled over to a patch of dirt. With delicate care, she tipped the bag in her hand and out rolled one of the seeds. Instantly, she thrust it into the cold earth and covered it up with her foot. "Now, you have three days…"

"Three days? For what?" My pounding heart thrummed loudly in my ears.

"Hush, child, and let me finish! You have three days to change your fate. But if you can't make this seed blossom into its intended purpose, you'll remain as you are for an eternity! For you see, this seed is to resemble your heart—if changed, it will sprout. If unchanged, it will remain dead, killed by winter's frost…but with feathers."

"I-I don't understand…"

"Ah, I almost forgot!" She snapped her fingers and flashed a wicked smile.

Instantly, I felt my insides burst from being suffocated and squished. The trees began to grow taller as the ground and I became acquainted. In a matter of seconds, I was buried under my jeans and winter jacket, trying to find a hole to breathe fresh air.

The world spun, and my lungs screamed. *What's going on?*

"Now, dearie, this is what will be your fate if you can't get this seed to grow; a hearty beanstalk it will be, too, if you are able. And since you can only cluck, no one can help you but yourself." She bent down to my level and plucked my body out from under the heap of clothes. "Some humility can thaw even the coldest of hearts and cause things to grow in the foulest of weather. Let's see if this little experiment changes things, hmm? You will know by the sound of a clanging bell if you've succeeded; it should reach you anywhere, but until then…"

She walked toward the edge of the woods, and in a blink, she was gone, her unfinished sentence still lingering in my ears.

Only three days.

Part Three

Currently In Duress

The sound of a car door slamming shut and footsteps echoing in the hallway wake me from my slumber. I can't remember when I closed my eyes, but it doesn't matter because I know what's next. The pan on the stove beside me sizzles with mixed veggies, the ones my mom usually sautés to go with the main dish—which I assume will be me. And the longer I try to analyze its contents, I realize that rosemary and sage will be my burial flowers. But then another scent catches my attention. The smell of recycled paper and leather circles about my nostrils, letting me know that my father is about to come around the corner.

"Any sign of her? I haven't received a call all day!" My mother rushes over to Father, grabbing his lapels.

"Not yet. I hung up more posters and asked everyone I saw in passing, made a few more calls. Still nothing. But those reporters are relentless. I wish they'd find another family's problems to obsess over." He runs his hand through his graying hair and sighs. The next moment, he takes a breath and lets his nose lead him into the kitchen. "Let's try to enjoy some dinner tonight and then go out later and keep searching." My father goes over to the stairs yet again and lets loose a holler. "Alice, Margaret, come down to help with dinner!"

Margaret rushes down the stairs, and still-sick Alice takes her time. My father goes up, I assume, to get dressed into comfy clothes and use the restroom. As the rest of my family scurries about the kitchen, I'm sitting in a large pot on the stove, thanking my lucky stars that my neck has yet to be snapped.

"Mom, why is the chicken still alive?" Alice comes over and stares into my eyes.

Shoot.

"Yeah, by now it's usually deboned and featherless. Why is it just sitting here?" Margaret walks over and looks at my face. Her head tilts to the side. "You know, its eyes kind of remind me of Anna's for some reason. Don't you think so?"

My mother walks over and takes another look at my face. Tears begin to form in the corners of her eyes, and I can't tell if it's because she can see the resemblance or because she is so hungry. Her look frightens me almost more than my impending death.

"Mom, what's wrong?" Margaret takes hold of my mother's hand.

"I just miss my darling baby! We all do. Even the animals are starting to look like her!" She bursts into sobs as she takes both of my sisters into her arms and hugs them.

Staring at them from within the aluminum pot two sizes too small for me, I realize how much love my family has for one another. And how much love they have for me. Why had I never noticed?

Footsteps are heard descending the stairs, and my mother and sisters break away.

Margaret turns her attention toward my father, who has just entered the kitchen. "Dad, you can do the honors this time." She takes out a butcher knife and hands it to him.

Fear rises in my thumping heart as I gaze at its glinting edge.

"Thanks, sweetie. We'll eat this chicken in honor of Anna because I know how much she would have loved to be here."

My gut twists at those words. Is that anxiety or guilt? Perhaps a little bit of both. My father is wrong—I wouldn't have wanted to be here. My family was always too overbearing, and being the middle child, I always got the short end of, well—everything; they never understood me. But this is different. I'm going to die, and there's nothing I want more than to be with my family, back in my human form, eating something other than myself.

All of their gazes turn toward me, but something outside the front window catches my attention. Someone dressed in a dark cloak is peering in through the clear glass, eyes like gaping black holes.

I shudder as recognition pummels me. The clock chimes the hour of eight, and the woman takes her sharp fingernail and etches the number four into the perfect glass. I can only assume that's how many hours I have left until I remain this way forever.

I glance back at my family to see if they notice the sound of scratching glass, but they never turn their heads. I look back at the window, and neither the old woman nor the number is there; have I lost my sanity?

It hardly matters now. I watch my father adjust his grip on the butcher knife.

He reaches into the pot and brings my body over to the cutting board. I flail and squawk, but his hold only tightens.

He puts down the knife and smooths his fingers along my neck, stretching it out just right. I wonder if he can feel my pulse beneath all the feathers. Would he recognize it as his daughter's?

If only I had been more loving. Why couldn't I have tried a little harder?

I taste salt and realize it's because of my father. Gentle tears are falling from his eyes, a rainfall of love as they splatter against the cutting board—love that had never faded, no matter how brutish I had become. Perhaps the Prius did drive as smooth as the Cooper. Perhaps the latest computer virus wouldn't destroy the entire internet if I just went out and did one chore. Perhaps if I listened, then I'd realize my family loved me, and that I loved them back…

My father takes a deep breath, ready to break the spine, but I keep hoping that I'll hear the bell signaling my freedom. To be cut short four hours is surely a crime against the code of magical conduct, but my complaints mean nothing.

As my internal countdown reaches one, a flash of green skyrockets into the air, tendrils snaking out in all directions as a stalk crashes through the kitchen window and wraps its vine-like fingers around my body. If squeezed any tighter, my bones might cave in on themselves.

I am hurled through the open window to the outdoors, the screams of my parents and siblings echoing behind me.

I hit the frozen ground, squeaking, a ripple of pain coursing through my small frame.

Then a deafening sound, like the chiming of the loudest, most out-of-tune bells, reaches my ears. A new pain follows, but it's not from the noise. My body convulses and writhes, my feathers falling out like hair follicles in the shower. Naked, cold, shivering. My body reshapes and arches itself into arms and legs. My spine stretches, and I cry out in agony, my clucks now sounding strangely human.

My vision clouds from the pain, the edges tinged in the deepest black until it fades altogether. The bells have grown faint now. I could have sworn I glimpsed a lock of my hair.

When I awake, I am on my back as familiar pitch-black eyes peer down into mine.

"Tis' a pity, dearie, you would have made a fine meal." The hag cackles and saunters away, snapping her fingers in the process. "My work here is done."

The old hag! What does she mean? I lift my hand toward my face and glimpse pale skin. Beautiful, featherless skin! *I'm human again!*

After being trapped in a chicken's body for three days, I find it hard to form words. I look at my naked state and am thankful the beanstalk's leaves are twice my size.

I fit one of the leaves around my body, and the beanstalk begins to shrink and sink into the earth from which it first came. Looking toward the house, I notice the kitchen window is no longer broken from the plant's entry. *Curious.*

The back door swings open, the one my mother had exited earlier to grab me for dinner, but this time it's Margaret walking out, a frown on her face.

"Anna, what on earth are you doing out here? And in the middle of winter?" Her hands are on her hips. "Are you…naked?"

"I…" My voice croaks like a frog. Who knew three days without talking could do this to someone? I tug the leaf to my chin. "Yes."

"I'm not even gonna ask why." She rolls her eyes. "Mom's making dinner, and Dad just got home from work. We're all inside waiting for you. You'd better hurry."

I find that I don't dread those words as much as I normally would. I'm actually…relieved?

Margaret looks me over once more and shakes her head. "You really are odd, you know that?"

If you only knew.

I follow her toward the house and step over the threshold, wrapping my makeshift covering tighter around my shaking limbs. "Mind if you distract everyone while I…put on some real clothes?"

"Fine, but make it quick. Dad's mouth is watering over Mom's new chicken recipe." Margaret almost walks away but stops short when her eyes settle on my head; she reaches out a hand and plucks something out of my hair. "A chicken feather? Really, Anna, you *are* peculiar." She hands me the feather and walks away laughing.

I can't help smiling. Perhaps being peculiar saved my life; it certainly humbled my pride.

The memory of pecking corn and eating bugs sends my stomach

roiling. That's something I *want* to forget. But these feathers?
I want to make sure I never forget why I got them.

16

The End

Crescent

(A mythical tale)

Along, long time ago, there was a girl who belonged to the sky. No, she wasn't born there, nor had she ever been to its heights, but she bore its mark. When she came into the world, everyone knew she was different. A small crescent sat below her right eye, a cream beauty mark branding her mocha skin.

She grew up wondering and wandering—restless—her gaze cast skyward. Her friends would scoff at her when she asked, *"Do you feel the sky calling?"* Others would laugh and run away without saying a word.

Her parents were gentle, but they too found it hard to understand. *"What of the fern? Or the squirrel's burrow? Do you see the earth's splendor?"*

The grass and trees were viridescent spectacles, the squirrels and chipmunks friendly, and yes, the golden sunlight joy itself, but there had to be more. Why else would she feel such a pull?

No one ever spoke of the evening and the lonely stars that lit the heavens. No one liked the night, for it bore shadows the sun couldn't cast away. No one liked the dark, and the girl knew it deeply.

She was one of the few who didn't fear it. Instead, she longed to understand it.

A cold dread settled about her like a cage, and she fled into the mountains to sit on the highest peak. On a rock, she pulled her knees to her chest and wept. The tears fell slowly and then all at once, like water breaking from a dam. It was growing dark, and at any moment the stars would be her companions.

She felt the wind. It picked up, swirling about her in steady gusts. She lifted her gaze, surprised to see wings flapping above her head. The wings were large and belonged to a wondrous barn owl as creamy white as the mark she bore.

"Why are you crying?" the owl asked, hovering before her.

"I feel stuck. And I don't know what to do," she said, drying her tears. But one still escaped down her cheek.

The owl stretched forth its wing and gently brushed the tear away. He paused and stared at the space below her right eye. *"You're a child of the sky. No wonder! Come, I have something to show you."*

The owl alighted on the ground and beckoned the child onto its back. Once secure, the creature shot up into the night and danced between the clouds.

A strange thing was happening. The girl felt something shift inside her—a tingling or a rush of anticipation. She'd never felt this way before—as if wings had sprouted in her stomach and longed to take flight.

The owl flew through the sky, circling around the stars. A constellation paused in his archery and adjusted his belt before greeting them. *"Welcome to the skies, young one. I am Orion."* He bowed. *"I have wondered when you would come. My brothers Castor and Sirius greet you as well. We hope you stay."* He resumed his pose and bent his bow once again.

The girl's smile widened; the creatures of the sky were friendlier than she'd imagined. What other secrets did this expanse hold?

The owl swooped and spun, reminding her to hold on tight. In the distance, a small speck of darkness devoid of any stars pricked her interest, and as they approached it, the darkness grew.

The girl wasn't afraid. Instead, she felt a strange calm. The darkness beckoned to her, and the owl seemed to hover just above it, waiting.

"This is what I came to show you. The abyss of the night. The lonely sky." The owl's voice grew solemn. He turned to look at her. *"And it's yours to fill."*

"Mine?" Surely this was a mistake. How could she fill the sky? *"I'm not sure I understand."* But she wanted to, more than anything.

"You are special, young one, and you have a gift unlike anyone else's. Use it." The owl called into the night, and in a matter of moments, other owls swooped in to form a circle around them. *"My*

brethren are here to help you."

Suddenly, a barred owl grabbed her right hand with his talon while a snowy owl did the same with her left. A tawny and a screech held onto her feet, their sharp claws surprisingly gentle on her skin. The barn owl flew around to face her, its knowing eyes beaming. She was stretched like a star in the dark abyss, surrounded by fluttering feathers.

She felt something deep inside her cry out in relief. She knew she belonged here. The cry echoed again. This was her space to claim. The longing and searching seemed to ease into a knowing as if she was made for this very moment.

A pinch of warmth, almost like a breath, alighted upon her face. The girl freed her hand from the barred owl's grasp and felt under her right eye, her birthmark burning beneath her fingertips. Then there was light, a kind so bright and unparalleled that it devoured the night.

The girl stretched out her hands and legs further, and the birds left their places, flapping their wings gently nearby. She was floating, alone, as tendrils of light snaked around her, wrapping themselves about her body and transforming her in all its brilliance.

When the light settled, the girl's face was radiant, filled with a certain brightness. But not the kind belonging to the light of day.

No, this was different. She felt it to her very core.

The owls hooted in applause; Orion, Castor, and Sirius hollered in joy. They thanked her profusely, lauding her with praise.

"What? What has happened? For I don't quite know what I've given to deserve this," the girl said amidst their cheers. She was finally free; she finally knew where she belonged, but she was still

lost. She didn't know yet what she'd become.

"Nay, little one. You have given us yourself—you've given us the moon."

The End

The Legend of the Lighthouse Keeper

(A mythical tale)

Since the dawn of time, there was a Great War. It waged between Land and Sea. For years, each sought dominance over the other, pushing and pulling against the borders, growing greedy in their need for power.

For a while, it was an even split, with the rampant tide pitted against the steadfastness of the shore. But soon, Land's strength began to waver, seeing as his shores grew weaker with each pounding wave.

Knowing this, Land sought a plan. He appealed to Sea's pride. "Draw back your waters. Your might is too great."

"Do you concede, then? Am I to be named victor?" Sea puffed out his chest.

Land swallowed hard—humility didn't come easy to someone as fixed as he. "I present a compromise…of sorts." A pause like a lingering breath.

Sea laughed. "Well? I'm listening."

Seagulls swarmed above, filling the silence with their mocking cries as if waiting to hear the verdict. It was evident they wanted the war to end so they could descend upon the waters and feed; with the churning surf, it was nigh impossible.

"You'll be named victor in exchange for something of worth," Land finally said.

Sea squinted as he stroked his smooth face, droplets of water dotting the air. "What is it you seek?"

"Your word—an ounce of your power. 'Twould be but a promise—a keeper of our agreement, should you relent." Land crossed his arms.

Sea arched a brow. "So I'll be deemed conqueror if I give you this precious gift? Crowned king of Sea *and* Land?"

"Aye."

"And what will you do? Gloat over it? Parade it around for all to see?"

Land shook his head. "Nay. I'll keep it hidden. It will be an aid to us both—locked away in a high tower just above the space where my shores meet your waters."

"And its purpose?"

"To remind us. When we see its light, may it keep us to our agreement."

"I abide by these terms. Agreed." Sea nodded and spun rapidly, creating a maelstrom that led to its depths. Out of its center emerged a blueish form as old and strong as Sea himself. When the form touched Land, it took the likeness of a young man.

Land constructed a lighthouse near the water's edge as he promised, and the young man was led inside. There he dwelt for the remainder of his days, growing aged and weathered to the tune of his masters, and kept the shoreline and wayward sailors safe.

He was a keeper of the light—the promise made between them: that Land should not encroach upon the waves, and thus, Sea should retain his barriers. And because of this keeper, Land and Sea dwelt in harmony the rest of their days.

The End

Coal of Smith-Harrow

(A *Cinderella* retelling)

"The magic won't last
So do have a ball
But beware and be wise
Or you might lose it all."

Chapter One

Once upon a time, in the faraway land of Glenfallow, there lived a young man named Coal Blackwood of the dusty town of Smith-Harrow.

Coal had a set of dark brown curls on his head, and his eyes were the color of midnight. He was strong and of medium build, standing as tall as six feet, but there was something unique about Coal that no one else in his village had. He was born with a crooked foot, and because of it, he walked with a limp and used a cane to get around.

Everyone in the village had watched Coal grow up and was used to seeing his wooden cane poking around door frames before his body followed suit. Coal, however, felt his difference keenly and was aware of the stares.

His mother had died when he was only eleven, and over the following years his father had taken to quitting his job and drinking out of grief. This prompted Coal to seek employment in town at the local blacksmith shop, where he apprenticed under Gris Bruback. There, he hoped to make enough money to support both him and his father.

It was at the forge where Coal felt most at home, for Gris Bruback was kind and wise, and his master didn't mind a damaged foot as long as the person had a working mind and two hands to do his labor. It was Gris who always encouraged Coal despite his limitations, proving to him that he was indeed worth something simply by hiring him.

But there was another uniqueness about Coal and his situation. For the smithy in which he worked had a window overlooking the town square, a place in which many gathered to sell their wares or to simply pass through to get from the Elm Woods to the castle. And it was here where Coal often looked out and saw Freya, as fair and golden as he was dark.

He had watched her grow up as one would a flower, sprouting slowly and then all at once into the most radiant of spectacles. It seemed both she and the flowers had something in common, for they both thrived in the sunshine as if it was their sole source of life.

But this particular flower was out of reach, only to be picked or chosen by someone other than him. For she was a princess, and he was a blacksmith's apprentice with a lame foot.

And it was from this very same window in which Coal looked out now and caught sight of Princess Freya entering town. She sat in a gold-filigree carriage pulled by Friesians of the slatest black; they could almost be a starless sky. The carriage rolled to a stop, and a footman hopped off the back to open her door. She was helped down the steps and escorted to the fountain in the town's center. Her dress was a light green, and her flaxen hair was pinned back to frame her delicate face.

Coal loved Mondays.

This was her early-week routine: Her bodyguards would let her sit in the sun as birds and children flocked around her. She'd greet them in kindness and tell them stories; it was always the sound of her voice on the wind that stirred Coal's affections deeper.

He'd seen so much of Freya's kindness—had heard her heart in the words she spoke—that her voice was as familiar to him as his own. Coal had loved her for as long as he could remember but had never found the courage to speak to her.

As Freya began to tell her stories, Coal continued hammering the broadsword lying on the anvil in front of him. But his eyes kept returning to her face.

"That's the easiest way to lose a finger, you know." Gris Bruback walked in, a pipe in his mouth and a knowing twinkle in his eye.

"I'm sorry, Master Bruback. It won't happen again." Coal shifted his gaze to focus on his work.

"I may be old, but I've been around long enough to know that isn't possible. You've been working here for the past eight years, and it's always the same. Why don't you go say hello to the lady and get it over with?" Gris Bruback suggested, putting down his pipe as he took a weathered apron off a hook and fitted it around his middle.

"She isn't something to just get over with, Master Bruback." Coal chanced another glance out the window. More children had come and were eager to listen to her stories. Freya never brought any books with her; she just spoke from her heart, and that impressed him all the more.

"Well, you'd better figure something out. I'm afraid if you keep waiting, you might lose your fingers *and* your head," Gris Bruback warned as he took his place by the fire, warming iron tongs in the flames.

As Coal thought about it, he wished more than anything to speak to Freya, to get to know her and for her to get to know him. Coal only wanted her if she'd have him in return, but who would want a man with a crooked foot? He hadn't introduced himself because of it and was too ashamed of his deformity to stand before her. Rejection from Freya would be worse than simply not talking to her at all. If only there was *some* way he could be made whole; only then would he find the courage to go outside and say something.

Coal continued to work hard into the evening, trying his best to focus on the tasks before him. Already he'd hammered two broadswords and was now working on a breastplate, but he still had some throwing knives and a set of pauldrons to make later. He had to get everything finished before the king's soldiers came for them tomorrow, and though Freya's beauty beckoned to him from the window, he'd be better off staying on task. His position depended on it.

By the time the sun began to set, Coal put the last throwing knife down amongst the others and wiped his sweaty brow with a rag. Gris Bruback was no longer in the smithy, having retired for the night earlier, and when Coal looked outside, Freya was gone, and the street vendors were closing their shops for the day. All that remained were some rock pigeons and wiley strays meowing for food amongst the remnants of day-old cabbage littered over the cobblestones.

Coal longed to see Freya once more, but it would be another week until she came back to town. And the more he sat and stared out the window, the more Gris Bruback's words seemed to haunt him.

"You've been working here for the past eight years, and it's always the same."

Coal felt the truth of it too keenly. Could he stand waiting another week just to see Freya's face through a window, too afraid to speak to her? Could he carry on in this same endless cycle?

He hobbled closer to the window and looked up, seeing a star more brilliant in luster and girth than he'd ever seen before. Something about the light stirred a longing in his heart. Coal had always dreamt of living a "normal" life, but now he was suddenly pining for it.

Something seemed to momentarily dim its shine as he gazed upon it, like a shadow had just passed before it or the heavens winked at him, but then the star shone brilliantly once again.

He closed his eyes, wishing with everything in him that things could be different, that he could be different—then maybe he'd have a chance with Freya. "Please," he whispered. "Even if it's just for a time."

But as he wished, no miraculous transformation happened. In fact, when he opened his eyes, he felt completely the same, if not a little more disappointed. But what was he to expect?

He was about to back away from the window when he heard a rustling in the hedge just outside it; he leaned closer and was startled to see a starling appear out of the shadows.

The bird perched on the window's ledge and seemed to observe Coal through the pane of glass, turning its head so only one of its eyes saw him at a time. It hopped closer to him, blinked, nodded, and then it was off and flying away into the night sky toward the glistening star.

Coal shook his head and turned from the widow, running a hand over his face. "I think I'm going mad." It *was* getting late.

He took off his apron, hung it on a peg, and locked up the smithy before making the short trek home.

Tomorrow would be a new day, and that held enough promise of its own. At least he hoped so.

Chapter Two

The morning came as quickly as the night had gone, so much so that Coal found he had overslept.

He rapidly got dressed and grabbed a peach before rushing out the door. He picked up his pace and ran through the streets, a lightness to his steps despite the adrenaline coursing through him. He'd be fired or hanged on the spot if the king's soldiers arrived before he did.

He was only a few minutes away now, but the sweat trickling down his back made it feel as though he'd been running for miles. But to his luck, as he rounded the bend, the king's men were riding along the cobblestones in the direction toward the smithy, not away from it.

He wouldn't lose his head this morning after all.

Coal quickly unlocked the door and moved with ease toward the bench of newly made armor and weapons. He held fast to the table, his chest heaving with every attempt to catch his breath.

Within a few minutes, the soldiers knocked and announced themselves, their large silhouettes filling the doorway with shadows, their horses tied up outside.

"Is the order ready?" the broader and more decorated of the two questioned.

"Yes, everything's right here." Coal motioned at the bench, and the soldiers walked toward it.

The decorated man grabbed the hilt of one of the broadswords and tested its weight before slashing the air in quick jabs. The other man picked up a pauldron, wrapping his knuckles against the metal. They both studied the quality of the items for a long moment.

"I'd like a word with the blacksmith who fashioned these," said the same man as he put down the sword. He scanned the room. "Is he here?"

Was the man jesting? Coal felt that he must be, but when the soldier's gaze alighted upon Gris Bruback as he entered the room, he moved to speak with him. "Good morrow, sir. Is this your handiwork?"

Gris Bruback had barely fitted his apron over his head when one of his eyebrows quirked up in surprise. "Oh, you mean the carefully crafted broadswords with the gold filigree inlay? No, I can't say I did that." Gris Bruback chuckled as he walked over to the forge and began kindling a fire in its ashy base.

"If not you, then who? Surely not…" The man turned around to look at Coal, scrutinizing him from head to toe.

"Ask the lad yourself," Gris Bruback shouted from across the room, hot tongs in his hand.

"Are you the maker?" the man questioned.

Coal's cheeks burned. What if the soldiers were here to complain over the swords? What if he did a poor job on the throwing knives and pauldrons? He'd just have to face the consequences; that's what he got for being half distracted by Freya's beauty.

"Yes, sir. It was my doing—all of it." Coal dropped his gaze to the dusty floor, awaiting a reprimand, when a firm hand gripped his shoulder.

"Never in my life have I seen such handiwork. I must say, I'm impressed. And that's no easy feat." The decorated fellow removed his hand but continued his speech. "I've been searching the neighboring towns and surrounding kingdoms for a good blacksmith, one I could have at my disposal to fashion weapons for my men. And to think, I've only had to look across the town square for the best. When the king suggested Bruback's Forge last month, I thought little of it. But come to find out he was right all along."

If possible, Coal's limbs grew weaker as he stood up straighter, the unexpected praise doing strange things to his body. Surely his talents weren't deserving of such declarations.

"As Captain of the Guard, I'm asking you to come live at the castle. There'll be work aplenty, and you'll find the comforts quite accommodating."

"Sir?" Coal mumbled, brows knotting.

But it wasn't so much a suggestion as it was a command, and Coal felt he didn't mind that in the least. In fact, he didn't know what to say. Last night he was pining for the woman he loved only to find that this morning he was being invited to live in her very home. Coal tried to digest this new turn of events when he was suddenly distracted by the horses neighing outside; they had grown uneasy. It wasn't until Coal saw a small, black bird flying around them that he understood why.

The soldiers turned to see the commotion.

"Philip, go check on the geldings before one of them tosses a shoe," the captain ordered.

Philip nodded and left the forge without a word.

Coal continued to stare outside as the bird left the horses and alighted upon the window sill; it was a starling, and Coal was convinced it was the same one that had appeared last night after he had made his wish.

But what was it doing back?

The bird whistled a strange tune, and Coal couldn't help but feel there were words embedded within—words only meant for his ears.

Upon a star-ling bird
You've wished, now see
Your fate that befalls you
Will come in threes.

Today's but a taste,
But tomorrow will dawn
And once it does
The show must go on.

Three days, three nights
You'll walk like a royal
A man with a purpose

Who no longer toils.

Until last stroke of twelve
That third midnight
Everything goes back
The same old plight.

The magic won't last
So do have a ball
But beware and be wise
Or you might lose it all.

The song ended as soon as it had begun, and the starling only stayed long enough to wink before flitting away.

Coal shuddered. What just happened? Had he heard the words correctly? Were they even words at all? A sense of foreboding prickled his skin to gooseflesh.

"What say you?" the captain questioned.

"Excuse me?" Coal had been so mesmerized by the bird that he'd forgotten about the man in front of him.

Right. The new job position. The castle. The king. Freya.

The man was awaiting his answer, and Coal didn't want to say no. But it wasn't quite that simple.

"What about my father? I can't leave him without money." Though the thought of not having to live in the same house as him bolstered Coal's spirits.

"Give us his address, and he will be properly looked after," the captain responded.

"What about my employer? Surely he can't afford to lose me; can you, Master Bruback?" Coal turned around to address the old man who had just walked over to join them.

"I'm afraid, Coal, that I can't afford to keep you. If the captain wants you, it's best you go." Gris Bruback placed a calloused hand on Coal's shoulder and smiled warmly. "But don't you fear, I'll find a replacement. My nephew Johnni will be in town soon, so perhaps I can persuade his mother to have me take him on."

It seemed that his fate was decided. His father would be taken care of, and his employer was giving him his blessing—there was nothing holding him back.

"We'll return to the forge tomorrow morning to collect these weapons and your things before we make the trek to the castle. It's not a long one, but the quicker we make the arrangements, the quicker you can get to work. You ride well, yes?" the captain questioned, gesturing toward the horses.

Coal stared blankly, his palms sweating. How could he answer this without looking like a fool? His foot hadn't allowed him to ride a horse before, never mind riding one *well*.

"Of course he does," Gris Bruback cut in.

"Then be ready by the morning." The captain gave a curt nod and met up with Philip outside. The men mounted their horses and cantered away.

The excitement of the new adventure now soured in Coal's stomach. How was he to ride to the castle? He'd make a fool of himself before even leaving the village.

"Thank you for coming to my defense," Coal said, "but I've never ridden before. My foot—"

Gris Bruback raised a hand, silencing Coal mid-sentence. "It looks like your journey to the castle isn't the only thing changing around here." He pointed to Coal's foot, a show of surprise on his face.

Sudden realization dawned as Coal looked down.

He'd been in such a rush to get to work that he'd left the house without his cane. He'd run through the streets! And miraculously, his foot wasn't even bothering him. Actually, it was looking quite straight.

How is this possible? Am I healed?

The words from the bird's song struck him anew. Perhaps his wish had come true after all. Perhaps he was finally becoming normal.

"If you'll only help me with a few things this morning, I'll give you the afternoon off to get yourself ready for tomorrow. You've got a big day ahead of you," Gris Bruback said with an air of somber pride.

"Yes, Master Bruback." Coal didn't know what else to say as he walked about the floor with ease.

He never imagined that a sturdy ankle could feel so much like hope.

Chapter Three

Never mind Coal's ankle, it was now his hands which felt twisted and strange. They gripped the reins of his horse like iron tongs to blistering metal, and they weren't relenting anytime soon. Not to mention his legs were glued to the sides of his steed—solely to keep them from shaking.

He never wanted to ride a horse again. Not if he could help it.

He glanced at the king's guard, all of whom eyed him curiously but otherwise seemed oblivious to his struggle. Either that, or they were secretly laughing behind their stoic expressions.

Coal fixed his gaze ahead; the castle was approaching, and despite his discomfort, a leaf on his newfound branch of hope unfurled.

Freya.

Just the thought of her sent his heart skittering against his chest. Would he get to see her? Now that he would be living at the castle, would he get to hear her stories as regularly as at the fountain?

He hoped it would be even more often.

"We're here," one of the guards said from beside him. "Get your head out of the clouds, boy, or you'll be minced meat before you lay your hand upon the anvil."

Coal gulped. He tugged on the reins, and his horse followed the others around the back and through a narrow entryway, which opened up into a wide expanse of green.

Soldiers of strong build and stature were fighting, drawing swords, and practicing lunges. A vein pulsed in Coal's neck. Though he was strong from his years at the smithy, even he didn't compete with the likes of these men.

The guard led him to the stables, where they all dismounted, and Coal breathed a sigh of relief. His legs were unsteady, but at least he was on solid ground.

A giant burlap sack was thrust into his arms before he had a chance to stabilize himself. The contact nearly pitched him backward.

"Follow me." The guard stalked out of the stable and motioned for Coal to keep up.

A few more steps outside and the man thrust open a wooden door leading into an outcropping of the castle. Within, the small room was tidy from top to bottom as if it was recently swept clean. A roaring fire blazed in the hearth, and an anvil stood nearby, outfitted with all the tools necessary to weld and bend even the toughest of metals. Another door was tucked away in the corner of the room, and a large window stretched across the back wall, overlooking what appeared to be a courtyard of sorts. And the smell…it held nothing of the acrid buildup of Gris Bruback's forge back home.

Coal felt his jaw drop. *This is where I'm to work?*

"His Majesty hopes you'll find your situation to your liking."

"To my liking?" Coal swallowed. It was more than to his liking. It was perfect. He'd never seen a more pristine workspace in his life. "You can tell His Majesty it's quite spectacular."

"You can tell him yourself. King Aldrich requests your presence in a quarter of an hour. Until then, make yourself at home." The guard shifted his stance, pointing to the closed door positioned in the far wall. "That's where you'll sleep. You'll find bedding in that bag." The guard nodded vaguely in the same direction he'd pointed and then left, the door banging shut behind him.

Coal was alone; all his thoughts were toward his impending visit with His Royal Majesty.

* * *

A knock sounded outside the smithy door. Before Coal had a chance at opening it, a guard stepped inside and said it was time to see the king.

The walk was long, but Coal knew it would have felt a lot longer had his foot not been straightened. As his body drifted through the gilded corridors of the castle, so did his mind drift toward thoughts of that elusive starling.

He thought he'd wished upon a star when, in fact, he'd had his wish granted by a bird. But that was all semantics, really. What mattered most to him now was that he was closer to Freya, if only by proximity, and he was going to see her father at this very moment.

His pace slowed.

The man looked over his shoulder and quirked a brow. "You all right?"

Coal nodded, but his footsteps faltered.

"The king might be powerful, but he is old and wise. Kind-hearted, I can assure you."

The guard's assurance did little to bolster Coal's nerves. He'd never stood before a king, let alone a king whose daughter he was in love with.

He nodded anyway and trailed the guard as they approached a set of two terribly large wooden doors. And when they were thrust open, Coal caught his breath.

The throne room was elaborate, to say the least, with navy and gold strung about everywhere, whether in the curtains, on the cushions, or embroidered into the robes. And upon the dais at the far end of the room sat an aged king, his salt-and-pepper hair a contrast to the dark bronze of his crown.

Coal stepped forward cautiously, unsure of how to act in such a royal presence.

"Is this the blacksmith?" King Aldrich beamed, his smile wide and inviting. Unlike the soldiers who had come to Gris Bruback's smithy yesterday, the king didn't appear shocked to see that it was a nineteen-year-old boy and not a forty-year-old man who stood before him. "Welcome, my boy!"

Coal dipped into a bow, keenly aware of the glares and speculative glances of the court. "Th-thank you," he said, his voice hoarse.

"I hope you find your accommodations pleasing," the king said.

Coal nodded. "Most pleasing, Your Majesty." In truth, he'd never seen a nicer forge. He'd never had his own room to sleep in, either.

"How grand!" King Aldrich clapped his hands. "Now, I bet you're wondering why I sent for you."

Coal remained silent; his stupefied expression likely said enough.

"It's no surprise that I run a friendly castle. We are the Frendleirs, after all." The king laughed at his own joke.

Freya Frendleir. It suited her.

"Because of this, I am hosting three consecutive balls for the birthdays of my dear daughters, Rina and Freya. They'll be sixteen, and all in the kingdom are welcome to attend."

"That's very gracious of you," Coal said. But what did it have anything to do with him, aside from the fact that his own traitorous heart was beating at the mere mention of Freya's name?

"And all who work under my roof are expected to attend." King Aldrich leaned forward, a gleam in his eye. "I know you are a newcomer, my boy, but you are expected, and cordially invited, to attend all three balls."

Coal tried swallowing the growing lump in the back of his throat, only to choke instead. He'd never danced before, had never been invited to a ball in his life. And he'd always had good reason; there wasn't much one could do with a lame foot, even if one tried.

"And, uh, when is the first ball, Your Majesty?" Coal asked. He'd have to prepare, after all—perhaps he'd take a few dance lessons. Oh, to see Freya again, to watch her glide about the dance floor in her elegant beauty! And to finally see her sister, who never came to town. He didn't know much about Rina, but the whole kingdom knew that she preferred horses to people.

"Yes, that is a good bit of information you ought to have, huh, my boy?" King Aldrich chuckled again. "The first ball is tonight. At six o'clock. So I suggest you shine your shoes."

Chapter Four

Tonight? Coal paced his room, his hands twining through his curls only for them to get snagged on his callouses. He had two left feet, and he would never appear properly dressed for such an occasion.

What was the king thinking? *Everyone* under his roof was expected to attend?

Suddenly, a knock sounded outside the smithy. Coal waited a few moments before it sounded again, this time even louder. And it didn't stop. He sucked in a breath and flung the door open, surprised to see a woman standing on his doorstep. She appeared to be in her early seventies, a basket of material and sewing needles in her arms. All Coal could do was blink down at her.

"Am I at the right forge? Or did I just get a whole lot older in the span of sixty seconds?" The woman crossed the threshold and laid her basket on top of an unused anvil, wiping her brow as she looked Coal over from head to toe. "You're a young one, aren't you?"

"Er… hello." Coal itched the back of his neck. Who was this woman?

"Well, let's have a look at you, shall we?" She motioned for Coal to spin around, but Coal wasn't one for spinning. He'd spent the majority of his nineteen years making sure he'd done anything but. For to spin would usually imply stumbling or falling thereafter.

She clapped her hands loudly. "If you want Frau Nannette to fix you up for the balls, then spin you must! Quickly, now!"

Coal spun swiftly, only to be stopped with a hand to his bicep. "Slower, slower! Do you want a concussion?" Frau Nannette whooped. "My needle and thread can only go so fast."

Coal acquiesced and made an effort to turn slower, feeling uncomfortable under Frau Nannette's prying gaze.

She tsked. "Just what I thought. Your legs are too long for your arms, and you have an uncommonly short neck for one so tall."

Coal shot her a scowl. He didn't appreciate the assessment, but he was too much of a gentleman to say so aloud.

"But no matter!" She waved a hand in the air. "I've been dealt worse—and with far less time, mind you." She hurried over to a stool tucked in the corner of the room and moved it in front of the large bay window next to the hearth. "Up you go!" She gestured for Coal to stand on the wooden platform, his legs wobbling in the effort.

She clucked her tongue as she took out a measuring tape and continued poking and prodding, this time with fabric in tow, all of varying shades and colors.

And just when Coal thought it couldn't get any worse, that he'd have to remain wobbling on the stool for all of eternity, Frau Nannette clapped her hands and stepped back.

"My job here is done." She swiped at her already dry brow. "I'll have these coattails and breeches snipped, stitched, and fixed within the hour."

Relieved, Coal let out a huff of air and stepped down from the platform. Surprisingly, his legs weren't as shaky as he'd expected.

The seamstress made for the door, ready to barrel over anyone who got in her way.

Coal cleared his throat before she could turn the handle. "Er…thank you." He didn't really *want* to thank her. She'd been intrusive and brusque, but she'd make it so he'd not stick out like a royal imposter in the evenings to come.

Frau Nannette dipped into a sarcastic curtsy and winked. "You're not so bad, urchin. Chin up; this royal frivolity may be just what you need."

And with that, she departed, her skirts narrowly escaping the door's mouth before it closed.

Coal stood in the new silence, heaving in a deep breath. What a whirlwind that woman was.

He had some spare time before the first ball, and he took a moment to admire his new forge. The walls were made of smooth, white stone, untouched by grime and everything the work entailed. He was told that the old forge burned down, and this new one was constructed and finished a few weeks ago.

Hence the urgency to fill it.

He could get rather comfortable in a place like this.

And all too soon, his heart dropped to his stomach.

Too bad it couldn't last. Hadn't the starling said as much? Though his foot was miraculously healed for the time being, he only had three days of normalcy.

Once the king realized he'd hired a cripple, Coal was sure he'd be packing his bags for Gris Bruback's forge the following day. It was only a matter of time.

"Better enjoy this while it lasts." He sighed, picking up a pair of iron tongs.

This was the first time in his nineteen years that he hadn't felt the pain of discomfort. Hadn't been the outcast. He'd been hired for his craftsmanship, his foot overlooked entirely. He'd learn to make the best of it and hope to see Freya at tonight's ball.

That thought alone bolstered his spirits.

He could endure a night of poor dancing for her sake.

He could endure anything if it meant being with Freya.

***

It felt like only ten minutes had ticked by when Frau Nannette invited herself back into the forge, her arms laden with freshly sewn clothes. She pushed past Coal and settled her garments on his cot in his bedroom, brushing out the folds and examining her handiwork like a proud mother.

Three half-jackets with coattails and matching breeches lay on his bed: a set of forest green, one of midnight blue, and another of deep burgundy. And the material looked far too expensive for someone like him to be wearing. Surely the king didn't mean for

Frau Nannette to outfit a mere commoner like he was a prince.

"I daresay, this is some of my best work!" she crooned, barely acknowledging Coal's presence. She turned to him then, standing in the doorway, her eyes glinting with humor. "You'll certainly look the part, I have no doubt."

Coal cleared his throat. "And what part is that exactly?"

She waved her hand at his question as if it were the silliest thing and proceeded to look inside the basket she'd plopped into a chair. She rummaged through the contents, humming every now and then.

"What are you doing?" Coal asked, trying to peer over her shoulder.

She spun, and in her hands were the shiniest pair of black loafers he'd ever seen.

"Are those…"

"For you, of course!" Frau Nannette thrust the shoes into his hands. "Didn't think I'd let you grace the dancefloor in those clobhobbers, did you?" She pointed to the ones on his feet, the leather scuffed horribly on his left insole where his foot had often dragged along the ground.

"I guess they've seen better days." Coal shrugged.

"Mercy, haven't we all." Frau Nannette threw her hands in the air. "But those shoes do take the cake." She gathered her things before brushing past him and out the bedroom door, pausing when she made it to the forge's exit. "Hurry now, you don't want to be late!" Like earlier, she winked and then left the smithy the same way she had come in.

In her wake, Coal was left wondering who else that woman accosted in the castle. She was a force to be reckoned with, and he feared he only knew the half of it.

Suddenly, chimes from the nearby cathedral struck the hour, and Coal listened intently to finalize the time. One…two…three… The bells chimed another three times in tune with his beating heart. It was six o'clock?

How had he miscounted? Hadn't it been four o'clock only an hour ago? His stomach dropped as he raced to get ready, Frau Nannette's words echoing in his head. He *was* already late. But better to be late than never show up at all.

He'd never gotten dressed faster in his life.

Chapter Five

The ballroom was extravagant, too luxurious for Coal's eyes, which were accustomed to the simplicity of dust and burning metal. He'd never seen such an array of colors before; even his burgundy coattails seemed to pale in comparison to the splendor. Skirts swished by him, hues of magenta and sapphire, and breeches of a similar nature joined them.

It was all too much.

But he had to be here. It was his duty.

Coal finally stepped over the threshold and entered the room fully, finding a seat along the far wall to bide his time. He searched through the extravagance for Freya; she was the true reason why he was here. He hoped to catch a glimpse of her and, if he was bold enough, actually approach her. Perhaps he'd even ask her for a dance.

His stomach grumbled, taking his mind off of the task. He'd

skipped dinner—breakfast and lunch, too, now that he thought about it—and he was paying for it. Eyeing a refreshment table on the opposite side of the room, he silently cursed his poor luck. In order to assuage the offending organ, he'd have to wade through the throng of guests.

Part of him wanted to run; the music was loud, the frivolity excessive, and the joy almost too jovial, as if no one at the ball had ever had a trial of their own.

And Coal knew trials. He lived one every day.

He stuffed down the discomfiture along with a deviled egg once he reached the refreshment table, hoping to ignore the pang in his chest.

"Did you hear the news?" a girl beside him whispered.

When he looked up to see who was speaking, it was to his relief that the conversation was directed toward a young lady on her other side and not himself. So he fixed his eyes on the table, gathering more food onto his plate as he listened.

"What news?" the other girl asked.

"About Princess Freya…"

Coal fought the urge to lift his head. *What news about the princess?* From the corner of his eye, he watched as the first girl leaned in toward her friend's ear, lowering her voice even more.

"She's not in attendance tonight. Has some sort of headache that keeps her abed."

Her friend's hands flew to her mouth. "The poor dear. And on her birthday ball, too." She shook her head.

"It's awfully kind that the king invited the entire village to these dances. Maybe tomorrow night we'll see her. Let's go find Rina instead!"

Seeming satisfied, the two girls sauntered off to join the fray. Coal fought off another sigh.

Freya wasn't here.

He was contemplating tossing his plate at the nearest server and making a dash for the exit when a hand grasped his shoulder. He turned, stunned to see the king behind him.

"Coal, my boy!" He beamed. "Welcome to the first ball!"

Coal dipped his head in a slow nod. "Th-thank you, Your Majesty."

"But what are you doing just standing over here? Tonight's a night of dancing!" King Aldrich prodded him forward, drawing him closer to the dance floor. "And there are many fine women just waiting to be asked to be swept off their feet." His eyes twinkled.

"Your Majesty?" Coal was having trouble wrapping his mind around dancing at all. He'd only wanted to see Freya; his plan hadn't accounted for actually moving about to stringed instruments—aside, perhaps, with *her*.

"Nights like these only come around so often, young man. Find a lady, take her for a spin, and enjoy your new station. You won't regret it." And with that, King Aldrich departed, finding a queenly woman standing near the dais and whisking her off at the start of the next song.

The king and queen looked the picture of perfection, but Coal only wanted to see Freya.

His heart couldn't bring himself to dance with another.

So he sat until the bell struck midnight and everyone departed for home.

***

The next night, Coal was prepared. Dressed in midnight blue attire, he had hope that things would go smoothly. More hope than he probably should.

This was only the second day, but he was determined to find Freya and introduce himself before his feebleness returned. He *needed* to.

That is, if she would even be in attendance tonight.

Skirting the edge of the ballroom, as he had done the night before, Coal found himself back at the refreshment table; there was something to be said about familiarity, after all.

He scanned the dance floor for Freya, trying to see a set of blonde curls bouncing amidst the music. But none seemed to shine as golden as hers. Instead, he saw her twin, Rina, dancing in the arms of a tall gentleman, a shy smile on her face.

Despite being twins, the woman looked nothing like her sister. Where Freya was light, Rina was dark. Freya was the morning, and Rina was the night. The contrast was jarring, but it only greatened his affection for her.

He'd fallen in love with Freya without having talked to her once. But she wasn't here. Again. And the thought nearly sent him reeling.

Coal took a step back, foot catching on something protruding from underneath the refreshment table. He fell on his backside, pain rippling through his tailbone as he noticed a pair of legs quickly retreating beneath the folds of the table skirt.

What in the world?

Curious, he lifted the edge of the material and peered underneath, stunned by what he found. "Your Royal Highness?"

"I-I'm so sorry! Was it you I tripped with my feet?" Freya asked, her eyes wide and glossy. Was she about to cry?

He moved underneath the table without hesitation. "It's no matter. I'm used to falling." Coal quirked a corner of his mouth, trying to show he was earnest, but her expression hadn't changed.

"Are you all right?" she asked again.

"Never better, Your Royal High—"

"Please, call me Freya," she said. "I don't much like titles."

Coal nodded but was too afraid to actually say her name aloud.

"Who are you?" she asked.

"My name is Coal. Coal Blackwood. I'm the castle's new blacksmith." *For now*, he didn't add. "But what—" How was he to phrase this? "What are you doing underneath the table?"

"Oh, yes. You must think me extremely odd." Freya shifted nervously. "I dropped something, and it rolled. I can't seem to find it, no matter how much I feel around for it." A blush climbed her cheeks.

Coal smiled, finding her blush rather becoming. "What did you drop? Perhaps I can be of some help."

Freya nodded. "Would you? I have no doubt your eyes are keener than mine." She laughed wryly. "It was a marble. A little gold thing with stardust at its core."

A marble? "Do you often carry marbles around with you?" Coal couldn't help asking as he searched the floor. It was difficult to see in the dim lighting, but that didn't stop him.

"No, only this one." She looked embarrassed, and Coal wanted to know why, but he didn't press her.

He spun on his hands and knees, still looking, when he saw something glint near the table's leg. He peered closer and retrieved the object. "I think I found it." He felt around the smooth surface of the orb, frowning when his thumb traced over a small knick. "Too bad it's busted, though. I think it broke when it fell."

Freya reached out her hand, and Coal dropped it into her palm, his fingers gently brushing her skin. A shiver shot through him, and he could have sworn she felt similarly if her deepening blush was any indicator.

She traced the marble with her finger, a satisfied smile lifting the corners of her mouth. "This is the one. Thank you! And don't worry, it's been broken for a while now. That's why it's one of my favorites."

Coal nodded, not quite understanding, but the mystery of it only added to Freya's appeal. There was still so much he didn't know about her, but he'd be satisfied to learn whatever she was willing to give him.

"Er, um…do you care to dance?" Coal sucked in a sharp breath as soon as the question left his mouth. He'd never danced before in his life—what was he thinking?

"Actually, I was hoping for a breath of fresh air." Freya bit her lip as if she was uncertain in the asking.

But it only alleviated the tension in Coal's chest. Outside he could handle. Miraculously enough, dancing would wait for another night.

"Sounds just the thing." He lifted a flap of the tablecloth and crawled out. "Come, I'll escort you." He gently grasped her hand and laced it through the crook of his arm, drawing her up to a standing position.

He half feared for all the stares they'd be getting, but no one seemed to pay them any attention. Relieved, Coal bypassed all the dancers and led her around the perimeter of the room. Eventually, he brought her to the double doors leading out to the balcony.

But he stopped before stepping foot outside.

"It's raining," he said, his hope deflating. The doors weren't open all the way, but they were propped to let in fresh air, enough to let him know the weather wasn't cooperating. "What now?"

"We bask in it!" She tugged him forward while her other hand found the door, pushing it open wider. And then she pressed on, stepping out beneath the overcast sky with a grin on her face. She grasped the balcony railing, directing her smile up at the heavens.

Coal caught his breath. In all his life, he had never seen a more beautiful and strange sight. He didn't know many women who loved the rain as thoroughly as Freya, and he was left wondering why it seemed to release unbridled joy in her.

"Aren't you afraid you'll catch a cold?" Coal asked, stepping out to meet her, drenched in the torrent the moment he left the safety of the indoors.

"No," she said, still smiling at the sky. "I've always loved the rain."

"Why is that?"

Freya's smile spread wider. "Because it makes me feel, Coal. Reminds me that I'm not alone. And sometimes that's enough, even when the world's grown dark."

Her words filled a void in his chest, shock running through him—and not just because she'd used his given name. Her declaration echoed a shared need—the need to feel seen, to be reminded he wasn't on his own, that the world wasn't only just filled with trial after trial.

But was it that easy?

Sure, his foot had healed temporarily, but what happened after? Was he ready to go back to a world of darkness once it went crooked? Living with his drunk father brought more pain than he often could bear, and knowing Freya wouldn't want to associate with him thereafter only drove the stake deeper.

The rain continued to fall, but it felt like icy daggers instead of the tranquil kisses Freya seemed to consider it to be. But he wasn't one to give up.

He closed his eyes, too, and tried to stop his racing thoughts. To just exist and be, come what may. He pushed the fear of his returning condition out of his mind and focused instead on the steady rain, enjoying the feeling of being still.

And it was then that the pelting grew gentler and his skin felt alive. He was beginning to understand.

There *was* a calmness about it. Freya was right.

It didn't diffuse his fears, but it was enough to quiet them, if only for the time being. Standing beneath the rain was freeing, like he was being seen—if not by the world, at least by his Creator. And that was a reminder he sorely needed.

Coal opened his eyes and cleared his throat. He glanced at Freya, shifting nervously on his feet. "Thank you," he said. "For this." He had never appreciated the rain more.

She looked at him now, though not fully, as if she was afraid to make eye contact. "You're welcome." She blushed again. "I find the rain is good for many things, one of them stripping us bare and reminding us we're all equals. For doesn't royalty stand beneath the same storm as the commoner, and the disabled the same as the abled? We are all the same."

Then the bell struck midnight once more.

Chapter Six

After a fitful night's rest, Coal woke early only to pace around the smithy, perseverating over Freya's words.

"We are all the same."

What had she meant by that? Surely she couldn't tell that he had a lame foot. The starling had assured him that the magic would last three days and wear off that final night. And yet she somehow said the very thing that cut through his facade and brought his heart peace.

Freya wouldn't judge him for his lame foot, but would she want anything more to do with him beyond friendship? Who would consider a husband a strong protector if he couldn't even stand?

Self-pity was the worst way to process his thoughts, but he couldn't avoid it as he moved from the smithy and paced around his bedroom instead. The third and final ball was to take place tonight—starting early and ending later than the previous two—

which meant this was his last day of normalcy.

A bitter pang twisted in his chest, but he stamped it down. He'd make the best of tonight, even if it was fleeting, for Coal sorely hoped to spend more time with Freya.

After their adventure in the rain had been disrupted by the chiming of the twelfth hour, the orchestra had wound down, and the guests left for home. Coal had wanted to talk to Freya further, but even he knew it was getting too late.

When they'd both reentered the ballroom, the king and queen hadn't seemed surprised to find them soaked from head to toe. In fact, the married couple shared a knowing look before whisking their daughters off to bed and bidding the rest of the company a good night.

The king had a glint of humor in his eye, mingled with something else Coal couldn't quite figure out.

His only consolation was the fact that Freya had seemed reluctant to go, and her blushing cheeks had indicated that she felt *something* in his company.

But *what* was the question.

He'd find out soon enough, but in the meantime, he needed to light a fire and hammer some metal.

***

For the third ball, Coal stood once more at the refreshment table, but this time in his forest-green coattails. He felt even more confident tonight, but then he saw Freya enter the room on the arm of a gentleman who looked as princely as Coal was not.

Were they…together?

His stomach dropped. He swallowed as he watched them descend the large staircase at the back of the room, her forest-green dress a perfect match with his own attire. Interwoven in the fabric were leaves and birds, trees and all forms of nature, and butterflies climbed the puff sleeves and neckline.

Despite his disappointment, he couldn't deny her beauty. She was utterly captivating; he only wished it was *he* who escorted her, his arm which hugged her close.

He tamped down his pride and walked in her direction, eager to claim her for the next dance. When he stood in front of her, the escort's gaze was passive, as if it was duty instead of love which motivated his actions.

Hope was a flighty thing indeed.

"Would you do me the honor of dancing with me tonight?" he asked. And feeling ever so bold, he leaned in and whispered, "Freya."

A grin split her features. "I had hoped you might come find me," she said, "but I don't dance. At least, not very well."

Coal's next words tumbled out of him faster than the rain that fell the night before. "Then we can try together. Come, I'll lead you."

He held out his arm to her and silently prayed he could carry out his promise. He had no idea *how* to lead, but he'd watched the other dancers the past two nights to know it involved a lot of guiding and lightness of foot, both of which he had limited experience in.

With Freya's arm looped through his, he led her to the dance floor. His hands were uncommonly clammy, his heart racing like a wild stallion, but those were small trials compared to the task at large. *Dancing.*

He gathered her close, one hand on the small of her back and the other holding her own. When Freya placed her free hand on his shoulder, time seemed to slow down, the room blurring in an array of tumbling colors.

And then the strings began, inviting them into a waltz.

Coal had no idea what he was doing, but surprisingly, it was working. The starling's magic must have granted his feet steadiness in all things, including dancing.

He spun Freya around the dance floor, her steps faltering every so often, but her grip and assurance secure. She trusted him, and that filled his heart more than words could say. Together they laughed, they talked and shared childhood stories, dreaming of simpler times, all the while twirling about the sea of waltzing people.

They danced every set, passing the night away in each other's company, ignoring the stares of curious onlookers. All Coal could think about was Freya and that he wanted to soak up every remaining second of his last day that would inevitably end in disaster.

And the best part? She didn't appear to want to leave his side either.

It was hours before Coal realized how long they'd been dancing, for the first strike of twelve seemed to shake the entire room awake, alerting his already pounding heart that time was up. His hope sank to his toes, but it was the realization that he needed to flee if he were to maintain any sort of self-preservation that made him nearly stumble.

The clock struck again and again, the countdown dwindling quickly.

"I-I must go." Coal choked out the words.

"Go?" Freya frowned. "So soon? Tonight's ball is to last longer than the others."

Part of him wanted to smile; he'd commandeered Freya's entire evening, and she was sad he was leaving. That thought alone tasted of sunshine, but when another chime struck the clock, it was as if the sun was covered in clouds.

None of this could last.

"I can't stay. I'm so sorry." Coal begrudgingly left Freya on the dance floor, his heart shattering at seeing her standing alone and confused. But he needed to go; if he had any chance of ever seeing her again, he needed to leave now. Not embarrass her on the dance floor.

So Coal fled. As he exited the ballroom, the last strike of twelve hit, and his foot snapped inward. Pain shot up his leg, and he fought the urge to cry out in agony.

Instead, his shoe snagged on the door, scuffing the insole terribly and ripping it off his foot as he tumbled forward. And down the staircase he fell. Thankfully, it was only a short flight, but it was enough to disorient him.

Shouts were heard from above, and he groaned as he pushed himself to standing, hurrying away from the chaotic scene.

If he was in any luck, he'd make it back to the smithy, strip off these fake clothes, and finally get to work as the blacksmith he was. Perhaps if he could prove he was still capable of working even with a lame foot, the king might keep him.

The thought brought little comfort, for it was unlikely at best.

The walk-limp back to the forge was a lot longer than he had anticipated. It was crazy how much one could forget in a matter of three days; his lame foot was foreign to him now, something he wished he could erase entirely.

When he finally made it to his safe haven, he threw himself on his bed and sighed deeply, no longer having the will to create anything. He'd wait until the morning to prove himself, to resume the role for which he was hired.

But tonight, the memory of the starling's words resounded inside his head, taunting him.

The magic won't last
So do have a ball
But beware and be wise
Or you might lose it all.

The bird had spoken more truth than Coal would like to admit. He really *had* lost everything.

Chapter Seven

The following morning, Coal awoke to the sun dancing in spurts across his face and a familiar voice calling his name. It was all sun and shadows beyond his lidded eyes, but when he finally opened them, he understood why.

The starling was outside his window, flitting in and out of the sun's rays, causing the shadows to flicker and writhe within his room. And the bird was speaking to him.

Coal, Coal, the day's come at last
My oh my, how magic dies fast
But get out of bed and face the truth
For one comes knocking, seeking you.

Coal thought he could understand the bird's words, but his brain was so muddled by a restless night's sleep that he wasn't sure.

Someone's coming...for me?

A knock sounded outside his smithy door, and it took every ounce of control for Coal to drag himself out of bed and not stumble from pure adrenaline, nevermind his crooked foot.

The knock came again, though it was much gentler than Coal would have imagined after an event such as last night. He had rushed out of the ballroom, leaving his beloved Freya alone and confused amongst a mass of people—on her birthday, no less. He regretted every part of it.

What on earth had he been thinking?

But he reminded himself it had been for a good cause; his foot would turn anyone away. But then why did guilt eat away at his core?

"Coal?" a timid voice asked beyond the door.

Freya? What was she doing here?

There was no use for it now. The truth would come out whether he continued to hide it or not; he just prayed she wouldn't hate him because of it. Or be too disgusted to even talk to him again.

He hobbled toward the door and hesitated, sighing deeply before opening it. Standing in the doorway was Freya, a bodyguard at her side, the man at least twice her height and nearly triple her weight.

"Good morning, Your Highness." Coal bowed, almost too shocked for words. He never imagined the princess seeking *him* out. But what stunned him more was what lay in her hands.

"I brought you your shoe." She smiled, holding the object close to her middle.

My shoe?

"One of the guards found it in the stairwell. So I…um…" She shifted on her feet. "May I come in?"

Coal was a blunderhead. "Oh, of course, forgive me!" He motioned for her to enter the room, acutely aware of her gaze as he shifted uncomfortably on his foot. Only, her attention was never drawn to his feet. Instead, she walked a few steps while still clinging to the guard, sitting once he brought her to the bench along the wall.

"If you'll excuse me, Your Highness, I'll just be waiting outside." The guard bowed but not before sending a piercing gaze that leveled Coal entirely.

Coal received the warning and nodded. He'd rather die than have something harm Freya.

Once the man left, Coal was more at ease, but only slightly. There was still the matter of his foot, and the woman he loved was soon to learn of it.

He debated on knowing how to start the conversation when she spoke first. "You ran away last night." She didn't look mad; instead she seemed hurt, the same hurt Coal had seen when he'd left her on the dance floor. "Can I ask you why?"

Coal's tongue stuck to the roof of his mouth, his hands clamming. Was he to speak the truth when her own eyes were ignoring what was right in front of her?

"I—" he tried. Swallowed. Clenched and unclenched his hands. "I was pressed for time."

"Time?" She tilted her head. "What do you mean?" Coal's shoe rested in her lap, and it didn't seem like she was ready to hand it over just yet.

"It was getting late," he said.

She pinched her brow as if she didn't believe him, but she didn't say as much. Then her eyes suddenly widened. "Was it something…" She paused. "Was it something I did?" She croaked the words out, almost as if she was too afraid to hear the answer.

Coal's heart cracked. He felt torn in two as he awkwardly knelt down in front of her and grasped her hands. "My dear Freya, absolutely not. There is nothing you could do that would ever make me run away."

"Then why…" Her voice quivered. "Why did you?"

She had him there. She'd called him out, and she deserved to know everything.

Coal silently cursed his foolishness. *Some birthday present I gave her.*

"I'm a broken man, Freya," he said, his shoulders slumping forward. "Surely you can see that." He gestured to his twisted foot, but her gaze remained fixed ahead.

"We're all a little broken, Coal."

"Not like me," he said, rising and hobbling around. It was time for the truth, whether he liked it or not. "See? I can barely walk with how crooked my foot is. I fear if you look at it for too long, you won't want to talk to me anymore. That you'll be repulsed by me."

She never looked at it once. Why wasn't she looking?

She straightened, eyes almost catching his. "Is that why you left? Because you were worried I'd misjudge you?"

"I've been misjudged my entire life; I've only ever wanted to be accepted. To be normal."

"And you?" She cleared her throat. "Would you judge someone if they weren't…*normal?*"

Coal stopped his awkward walking demonstration and paused. Would he? He'd only ever wanted to know what it was like to have a properly functioning body. And he'd been granted that by the starling, but had it really changed anything? He hadn't acquired any stares, true, but he knew the magic wouldn't last. Nothing good usually did, as was his case.

But maybe that mindset was wrong.

He already knew his answer. He wouldn't judge anyone for being different. He knew how it felt, had tasted normalcy, and knew what it would be like to have that stripped away. Anyone in his position deserved a chance, like Gris Bruback had given him. Like Freya was giving him now.

"No. I wouldn't," he said. "Though I can't imagine anything worse than this."

Freya sighed, a small smile pulling at the corner of her mouth. "You still don't realize it, do you?"

"Realize what?" he asked, searching her face.

"I'm blind, Coal. I have been ever since I was born."

Blind? Balderdash. Was she serious?

And here he was complaining about his foot! Guilt niggled the back of his mind, and he felt tears threaten to spill from his eyes. How had he not noticed before? He'd been too struck by Freya's beauty to see it: the glossy eyes, the often vacant expression. They were all there now, but he'd only ever viewed them as part of her appeal. Her beauty. Nothing, *nothing* could ever dull that.

"That's why you never looked at my foot. And all this time…" He sat next to her on the bench. He combed his fingers through his hair as he leaned forward on his knees.

"All this time?" she asked.

"I'd wished upon a starling to heal me, to make me confident enough to approach you so I'd be worthy of your presence." Coal laughed at how ridiculous he sounded.

"A man is worthy of anyone's presence by what's in his heart, not by how he walks," Freya said softly.

"I'm so sorry you have to deal with this, Freya."

"Don't be." She smiled. "I've been given a unique perspective. To judge based solely on character and not appearance. It's a gift, Coal, and one I wouldn't trade willingly."

Coal marveled at her. Not only was Freya beautiful, but her heart was even more so. She had struggles like him, if not worse, and she'd chosen to embrace them rather than become a pariah of society.

"Do you think…" He cleared his throat, not quite knowing how to proceed. "Do you think your father will let me stay here?"

Freya turned to him and finally handed over his shoe, smirking. "Only if you promise to keep your shoes on when you work."

Coal burst out laughing, taking the offered item and letting his hand linger on hers. "And do you think…" He cleared his throat. "Do you think I could ever have a chance at winning your heart?" A presumptuous question, if not a little dangerous. But he'd rather risk it than not ask at all.

Freya lifted a brow. "You're not a cave troll, are you?"

Coal reached over and brushed his fingers against her cheek. "No, just an ordinary one."

"Good." She grinned again. "I can't stand caves." She squeezed his hand and started laughing.

They both did. Laughter filled the smithy like smoke often did, but this was much more pleasant.

And they remained that way until lunchtime, when Freya, who was a steady crutch for Coal, and Coal, who was Freya's eyes, proceeded down the castle corridor hand in hand.

It was the makings of a beautiful beginning.

The End

Adventure

Stories in the Dark

(A nautical tale for children)

And the hollowed ship swayed back and forth, back and forth, back and forth, back and…" Graidy's mother moved him in the direction of her words as laughs burst from his mouth. Her long, blonde hair brushed the sides of his cheeks, and her blue eyes glimmered.

"I get it, Mum! Keep going!" Graidy smiled. The cabin's lone flickering candle cast dancing shadows against the opposite wall and window pane behind him.

It was raining outside, as Ireland was prone to do. And from his small cot tucked cozily near the window, Graidy heard the faint pitter-patter trickle off the thatched rooftop and saw the droplets fall like little diamonds in a mine shaft outside. The window showcased a world of clouds, suffocating the natural light and making way for that of man-made fire. The trees outside loomed like tall, dark soldiers, serving as a barricade against high winds.

"It's all part of the experience, Graid. Yer Mum is quite the storyteller," his father said from across the room. "Oh, yer shoulda' heard the stories she'd tell me before yer were born! She has a way of makin' 'em come ta life." Seated on a three-legged stool, his father peered from behind a pair of blue-rimmed spectacles over a weathered *Moby Dick* to show a toothy grin. The yellow walls around him became a deeper hue in the orange firelight, adding a dimension of warmth to the small room.

"Declan, my stories of America hardly count. You just find anything that's not from *here* amusing." She gave him a teasing glance and returned her attention to Graidy, gazing into his deep blue eyes; he was told they resembled the sea. "Graid, you ready for some more of the story?"

His numerous head nods and fidgeting body sent the shadows behind him into a wild frenzy, as if the walls were eager to listen, too.

"Okay. Where was I…? Oh, that's right…and the ship swayed back and forth, but the crew tried to hold fast as their captain issued out commands: 'Steady the starboard side! Secure the anchor! Make ready the harpoons! Gentlemen, we are preparing for battle!'"

"Mum, why are they going to fight?" Graidy's eyes widened as the shadows on the walls began to resemble waves; his small cot started to sway underneath him as little patches of glistening light formed all around him. The teakettle on the stove began to take the shape of a bird, and the wooden stirring spoons hanging on wall hooks underneath the cabinets started to look like small krill. Enthralled, he leaned in closer to hear more.

"You see, Graid, Captain Horatio MacCallin had been cursed by Sir Roberts, a crew member he marooned on an island for committing treason. Little did he know of Roberts' dealings with the Dark. The man had pulled Captain Horatio aside and threatened that to travel by ship would be his death, that he and his crew were never to receive safe passage across the seas again. Thus, Captain Horatio became a landlubber. But after four long years of living in fear, he decided to take his chances. He rounded up his crew to embark on the waters once again, the lot of them unaware of the circumstances and him only guessing what was to be their fate. That brings us to this very moment." Graidy's mother twirled a lock of hair around her fingers, as engrossed in the story as Graidy. And she was about to continue had it not been for the laugh coming from his father's direction.

"What's so funny?" she asked. Both she and Graidy looked at him, his full beard split by a grin of shining teeth.

"If ye keep tuggin' at those golden locks, yer gonna' be bald, Kate. But don't let me int'rupt; yer gettin' to my favorite part." He winked and went back to his novel, fixing his green eyes and blue frames once more on the pages before him. But he had hardly a moment to read when he was hit square in the head.

"Oh hush!" Graidy's mother gave him a teasing glance as a pillow bounced off his temple and tumbled to the floor.

Graidy couldn't help laughing.

His father picked up the offending object and used it to prop his arms. "Thank you, love. How'd ye know I needed this?"

Graidy watched as his mother rolled her eyes and tried not to laugh at his father's unaffected remark. They would do this often—playful banter—and Graidy always found it fascinating. Eventually, his mother returned her gaze to him and continued the story.

"As I was saying…the seas were raging and rising, spilling onto the deck and even sweeping one of the crewmembers off his feet and over the side of the ship. Something was coming. The captain and his crew grew frantic as they felt the swells grow in height, the sound of the waves slapping the hull like that of splintering wood. Faint, low cries could be heard in the distance, and no one wanted to question what it was. The captain yelled, 'We got to get the youngster out of the water before it's too late!' as the storm began to grow wilder and the low moaning became more consistent."

Graidy looked away from his mother and noticed that, though his father's eyes were directed toward his book, they were now closed, scrunched slightly as if in deep concentration. It appeared he, too, was engrossed in the story and would rather hear one than read one himself.

The rain began to fall harder, splashing in through the window and leaking through cracks in the ceiling. The shadows reciprocated the rain and splashed about the room, too, seeping under the furniture as the little glistening pools of light transformed into giant puddles of dark, gray liquid. They writhed and danced all the more, casting feathered silhouettes against the walls before being overcome by waves of gray. *Are the shadows…squawking?*

Graidy quickly moved his dangling feet and placed them atop his covers just seconds before the mysterious water touched them. *What's happening?*

His parents didn't seem to notice, nor did the candle stop burning once it was fully encased in liquid. But it didn't matter; the water reached his sheets and clothes, and he could feel his body begin to rise, floating upwards. And just like a creature coming up for air, Graidy broke through the surface of the thatched roof, released onto the open sea in the midst of a terrible storm. He flailed about the water, trying to stay afloat, for he hadn't yet learned how to swim.

"Aye, there he is! Sylvester, prepare the dinghy and make haste! The child's about to drown!" the captain barked as he took a harpoon, a net, and three other crew members to join him in the rescue mission. "Gentlemen, we can never be too careful; be on your guard, ready to strike at any moment!"

Graidy did his best to keep his head above the water while the men were on their way, but the waves were getting bigger and the rain was only falling harder. And yet sweet relief met him as he was snatched up onto a wooden boat, coughing out copious amounts of swallowed water. After disgorging the ocean, he received a blanket from one of the men and was a bit more at ease, though he couldn't say the same for the barn swallows. He *had* heard birds after all! With gaze lifted, he watched as they circled the overcast sky as if signaling a warning, clearly disturbed over something.

But what?

Glancing at his rescuers, he recognized the familiar faces of those he had seen in past dreams or in the waking world, so much so that even the captain's green eyes resembled his father's, but this man had a peg leg.

A high-pitched, whistling tune arrested his attention; the

contrast was jarring with the low moans that steadily grew nearer. It didn't take Graidy long to realize it was coming from the captain, whose lips puckered slightly in a funnel-shaped way. While he whistled, his crew navigated the wooden oars through the waters, and in a short time, his whistles became the words of a song:

We row to tow our kins
Upon the blisterin' winds
Seekin' out lost treasure
Cost to be our pleasure
(whistles)

When Sir Roberts, our own
We marooned and disowned
For his crimes of treason
The worst kind of heathen
(whistles)

His dealings with the devil
Cursin' the Seas as evil
A Monster birthed from hate
We await our bitter fate
(whistles)

The captain ended the song with more whistling, and Graidy was left puzzling over its meaning. But he didn't have much time for that. They were nearer to the ship, but the deep, low cries were so close now that all the crew shook in fear, including Graidy.

"We're almost back to her! Keep rowing before the beast swallows us whole!" the captain urged, but before Graidy could question what the beast was, something swam beneath their boat, jostling the small craft and causing everyone to lose their balance.

"What was that?" one of the crewmembers asked, his face pale.

Graidy peered over the edge of the boat, and all he saw was dark liquid masking any signs of what had just passed under them. But he did notice how the air had grown stale despite the heavy rainfall. Something was about to happen, and he had a feeling it wouldn't be good.

Even the barn swallows seemed to understand. Their calls became more frantic as their little bodies darted through the pelting rain. He'd learned from his mother that they symbolized a sailor's return home. But would any of these men make it home after this?

Graidy hadn't any clue what lurked below the seas, but he wondered: Would the barn swallows be a good omen of his return, too?

As the captain tried to calm his men, a large creature broke through the surface of the water in front of them, blocking their path.

The crew erupted into panicked shouts.

The creature roared, revealing at least five rows of pointed teeth. Following the body, a set of eight writhing tentacles shot skyward, towering over them like a fortress of trees barricading a castle. And then they dropped, slapping loudly on the water like raindrops on a rooftop. The flailing tentacles mixed with the falling rain until the whole earth felt like it was shaking. And the monster appeared to be waiting before it lunged.

"Blimey, it's a kraken!" the captain shouted. From his tone, it was evident that this wasn't just any monster. It was one from the depths.

Gooseflesh climbed Graidy's skin; he wanted to run and hide.

The crew crossed themselves, sending up prayers for their lives.

"Stand back, you foul beast! Men, take heart and fight!" the captain said.

But the crew, struck with terror, foolishly abandoned the boat and began to swim. All at once, the icy depths took them and sent them drifting away.

"Where are you going? Come back!" Graidy called after them. But his strained cries were muted by the roars of the hideous creature.

Particles of saliva mixed with rainwater splattered against his face as a foul stench reached his nose. Instantly, his gaze climbed to the monster's eyes—soulless windows of flickering candlelight, all ferocity and no warmth.

Graidy stood frozen in fear.

"If only this were the beasty which stole my leg," the captain shouted beside him, gritting his teeth. "I'd much prefer the whale." He set his jaw and looked at Graidy. "But we can't change that now, can we, lad? We've a date with the devil, and I aim for us to come out alive. Take this and wait for my signal." The captain thrust the net into Graidy's hands while he readied the harpoon. A pair of blue-rimmed spectacles fell from his pocket, and his peg leg crunched them underneath his weight.

Graidy wanted to salvage what he could of them; however, now was not the time. Dread still pooled in his stomach from hearing the captain's orders. He had no cause to fear the kraken and his fiery eyes, right? With shaky legs, he stood his ground and prepared for action. By now, the monster looked like it was ready to attack.

"All right, my boy, on the count of three. One…" the captain began.

The monster roared and reared, causing the waters to quake.

Graidy could feel his body sweating underneath layers of fabric despite their already sodden state.

"Two…" The captain prepared the harpoon, his hand on the trigger, ready to fire.

In one swift motion, the kraken shot out two tentacles which came down mere feet from the small vessel; a resulting swell pushed the boat skyward.

Temporarily having the higher ground, the captain let loose the harpoon and hit home in one of the kraken's fiery eyes. "Three! Now, lad!"

Graidy, not sure what to do, swung his arms back and sent the large net flying. It unwound and landed on the red-eyed beast, covering most of his head and body. Graidy yanked the ropes taut.

The kraken fumed as its angry cry rent the air. The creature swayed back and forth but was unable to get away. Even with its sharp teeth, the beast gnawed unsuccessfully at the net, next attempting to pry it off with its tentacles, but the captain let loose another harpoon, and this time hit the monster square in the heart. The beast writhed in agony, trying once more in vain to escape, but to no avail. The body fell forward and crashed into the small boat, breaking and splintering the wood into tiny bits.

Both Graidy and the captain were left floundering amidst the churning sea.

Graidy needed to stay above the surface, gasping for air and searching for something to cling to, but as he saw the captain slip farther and farther away, he began to grow weary.

"Captain! Where are you going? Is that it?" But his question merited no response. Waves forcibly swept over him, pushing him downwards, and no matter how hard he struggled to stay afloat, he kept sinking deeper and deeper below the surface. The rain had calmed, the sea had stopped raging, they had won, but Graidy was too focused on falling.

He fell for what seemed a long time as he tried to conserve his last gulps of air by holding his breath and closing his eyes. He was about to give up until his body hit something soft and fluffy underneath him.

"Graid, what are you doing?"

Graidy felt a soft hand stroke his chin, and he carefully opened one eye at a time. His mother was staring at him, a bemused look on her face.

I'm alive. The kraken didn't get me. I'm back home.

In that same moment, he expelled a long breath and quickly sucked in a new one. He didn't realize how tightly his fists were clenched until he stretched his fingers in the cozy fabric of his bed, returning feeling back into them.

"Did you like the story?" his mother asked, a sparkle in her eyes.

Graidy felt his face, his clothes. *Dry. Everything's dry. What just happened?* "Where did the captain go? Where's the rest of the crew? Is the ship okay? Did the…"

"My goodness, you have a lot of questions!" She laughed and looked back, smiling at her husband, who was now standing up and heading over to their bed in the corner. He put down his book, grabbed the pillow, and took the still-burning candle and placed it on Graidy's nightstand. His footsteps created small creaks in the floorboards as he shuffled around his bed.

"Perhaps there'll be a follow-up story tomorra night," his father said with a wink.

"But I wanna know now… Mum, Da!" Graidy looked from one parent to the other, hoping to get an answer.

"Some things are best left ta the imagination, Graid. Goodnight." He chuckled, ruffling Graidy's hair. "Goodnight, love!" He bent down and kissed his wife soundly on the lips and took his place on the bed, leaving the side closest to his son's cot open for his wife. He rolled over onto his back, and in a matter of moments, gentle snores were already escaping his mouth.

"Your father's right, and you have quite the imagination! Now it's time for some sleep." Graidy's mother gave him a warm smile and a kiss on the cheek before moving to close the window above his cot; though the storm had settled down, it was best not to allow any more rain inside.

But as she began to close it, Graidy saw a barn swallow dart from the trees and alight on a bush by the window. It called into the night, its twitter-warble song a comfort that maybe the captain from the story had made it home safely. Just like Graidy had.

"Look, Graid, I believe she came to bid you goodnight," his mother said, pointing to the bird.

Graidy smiled.

And just as soon as the swallow had come, it flitted away with the resounding click of the window being shut. His mother's shadow danced in the flickering candlelight, and Graidy couldn't help but be reminded of the story and the shadows of the raging sea.

She made her way to her side of the bed, whispering, "I love you," and reached to blow out the candle. But before the light went out, Graidy noticed a familiar pair of broken blue spectacles on the ground underneath his father's wooden stool.

And he only had to wonder.

Much like the swallows, perhaps the captain really had come home after all.

The End

The Tale of Markhus Roder

(A *Robin Hood* inspired tale of forgiveness)

Adrenaline pounded in Rin's ears, and her breath came short and ragged.

Up high in an evergreen, she sat tucked away in an alcove of three medium-sized branches, feeling like a bird in her nest, though much sappier and not quite as safe. An overhang of cone-like needles shadowed her view of the sky, but the sun was resilient and penetrated their cover.

Rin had grown up hearing about Irindel's Bluff, home of the infamous Everwood forest, and now that she was finally here, it was safe to say that she loved it. Very much. Here it was warm, and she felt close to the sky.

Vastly different from the cage she was used to, this forest

boasted freedom.

But it was only a matter of time until she was found.

*****

Rin's residence in Hawksbrooke had been her home for her entire life—nineteen years, to be exact—but she much preferred the Everwood with its unwavering greenery during the ever-changing seasons. It was so unlike her current abode, cold and made of stone; the monolith in which she had lived was gratuitous. Whether scoffed at or admired from a distance, the sleek, gray infrastructure with its countless turrets and gothic-style windows was a sight to be seen. Pillars of marble accentuated the large, wooden entrance as flying buttresses jutted from its walls.

Outside was magnificent, but it was inside where the true beauty flourished. Colors of deep crimson and royal blue, majestic purple, and living green were in every drapery, floor rug, and cushion. Large tapestries of soldiers, rulers, and past generations hung about the many corridors—all signs of fortitude—while mahogany flooring stretched from room to room and ascended the staircase. Bouquets of orange lilies and yellow marigolds were stationed at every turn while a bountiful cornucopia sat on a long oaken table in the Great Hall.

The best maids, cooks, seamstresses, carpenters, and the like all lived in the lower bailey within Hawksbrooke's walls, given that they worked under strict orders; they were told to be grateful because of their fortunate position, and most were. The establishment was a dream, everyone said.

Everyone except for Rin.

Growing up in Hawksbrooke brought its challenges, and there were too many rules to suit her free-spirited nature. She was told what a fortune it was to be born into such "good" company—the king was her uncle, after all—but one of the only things she enjoyed about growing up were the stories her father told her before bedtime.

"Is it true, Papa? Did Markhus Roder really help them?"

"Every last one of 'em! And he got the best of those inconsiderate snobs, too. The valiant Markhus fought for justice, giving food and money to the poor."

"Don't forget about Fidget!" Rin chimed in. *"He helped, too!"*

Her father winked. *"Of course. One could never forget Markhus' trusty hawk."*

A stream of giggles erupted from Rin's mouth as her father stood tall and proud, looking ridiculous with both a wooden sword in his hand and a quiver of arrows with a long bow strapped on his back, gesturing left and right as if to reenact the heroic scene. A stuffed red-tailed hawk, playing the part of Fidget, perched on his shoulder. His brown eyes and auburn hair danced in the candlelight as he exaggerated the more intense parts of his charade, an aspect of his storytelling that always made Rin smile.

Her large, green eyes and inky black curls were quite the contrast to her father's features, but she was told she got her looks from her mother, and it was confirmed whenever she'd glance at the painting of her parents resting on her bedside table.

Her father finished his performance by reaching behind Rin's ear and producing a bright gold coin. *"And it happened just like that."*

Rin's already large eyes opened a bit wider at the sight of such a shiny object. It wasn't any ordinary coin; from the imprinted hawk in the metal, she knew it was a coin of the rebellion, Markus Roder's trademark, stamped in secret. Few of those who were loyal to his cause were bold enough to carry them on their person.

Her father placed it gently in her hands. *"Now, hold onto that so you'll never forget these stories; guard it well, Little Rin. And promise me you'll never leave this place. It's not safe out there. The king's guard can be most...unforgiving."* Her father, though still smiling, choked out the last word as if he'd just swallowed something too large for his throat.

"I won't forget, Papa, I promise."

And she hadn't. As Rin continued to grow older, she was told fewer and fewer stories, but every time she glanced at her coin, she'd remember them all. Both the happy and the sad. The stories that filled her heart with joy and longing, and the ones that made her toes curl and fists clench tight.

The latter was the most vivid, for she'd recall the stories of beggars who lived on Sherwoode Village's streets, scrambling to find sustenance for their families, while there were those who mocked their existence and made a living at their expense. And no matter the attempts at charity, it was all for naught.

"There was once a man who went to market with a plan," her father began. *"He purchased six fresh trout, a wedge of pepper jack cheese, and four loaves of pumpernickel bread in hopes of giving it to the poor. The vendors sold him the goods, unaware of his*

intentions, but once they saw him giving it all away, they grew fearful." Her father shook his head. *"If the king found out that they were the ones responsible for selling the man food in order to feed the hungry, then surely they'd lose their jobs, or worse. Be sent to prison."*

Rin couldn't help scowling at the cruelty of it all.

"And with their greatest fears confirmed, the Royal Guard came through Sherwoode Village, interrupting the illegal feast with their leader grabbing the man by his collar. 'You know the punishment for such a crime. Everyone has to work for a living. No one gives free handouts without the jurisdiction of the king!'

"'If I may, sir,' one of the poor women spoke up. 'Many of us have tried to work; no one will hire us. And there's only so much mending arthritic fingers can do.' She gestured to her hands. 'This charitable man was only doing an act of kindness, one that will save many lives today.'

"The leader scoffed. 'You know the rules. You all know the rules.' Without a second thought, he gathered the food in his arms and nodded to his comrades. 'Find out who else is responsible and shackle this man in irons,' he said, looking at the charitable giver before walking away.

"Thus, the man who bought the food and eventually the vendors who sold it to him were all sent to prison with the warning that further actions of the same nature would lead to death.

"The king's verdict was justified because he was king, after all, and he never listened to anyone's advice, not even his own brother's. Things were starting to look bleak, but then something happened."

"What, Papa?" Rin asked, unsure whether she should still feel angry or not. Her father had that telltale twinkle in his eye, so she knew not to fear.

He cleared his throat. *"The next day, the vendors were all freed, the poor got their food, along with a bag of coins for each family, and half the Royal Guard woke up with bald heads and holes in their trousers. Everyone claimed that it was the work of Markhus Roder and his hawk, who, one clad in a midnight cloak and black leather gloves and the other as brown and mottled as tree bark, had set things right before fading back into the shadows of the Everwood."*

As a child, Rin had wanted to believe from the depths of her soul that Markhus was real, and from her father's constant stories, it seemed quite possible. But the more she thought about him, there grew a longing to catch him and Fidget in action, to leave the confines of her home and seek the truth in all the stories she had been told.

But behind her father's freeing words was a cage of captivity, for he wouldn't let her leave the house out of fear that it would be too risky; she'd learned that at a young age. But it hardly seemed fair—what was so dangerous about leaving the castle?

She often asked why her mother had been able to leave the grounds whenever she had wanted to—she'd heard the stories—but her father's reply was always, *"It was before you were born, Little Rin. Times were different then."* It was never the answer she had hoped for. Every time she would bring it up, her father would become distant and quiet, so she figured there must be a correlation between the two—some secret he was trying to evade.

In the end, he would restate the importance of her staying indoors, saying it was her duty to fill her mother's shoes. Rin knew it was more than that, though—she was told her mother had passed away when giving birth to her, and secretly, she felt her father resented her for it, though he'd never say so.

The idea became too great a burden for Rin to handle and had only prompted her to find a means of escape all the more. To seek the truth.

And as she grew older, her perspective shifted. Her desire to leave home was not only based on finding Markhus Roder but on finally tasting the freedom she craved. Rin wanted to be away from the royal household, and if her father wasn't going to let her out of the castle grounds, then she'd let herself out. She was tired of being locked up, and no handsome prince was coming to set her free because she'd never had the chance of meeting one.

She had to take matters into her own hands.

***

The current thumping in Rin's chest brought her back to reality.

Nineteen years had passed, but she had finally done it. She'd finally found her courage and ran away.

It had been easy, really. After thoroughly surveying the layout of the castle, she figured out the best time of day when the Royal Guard was short-staffed. It only happened once a year, during a holiday the king coined "The Glory Feast," which was exactly as it sounded: the celebration of the king's wealth and all he could afford to eat. At least he was gracious enough to annually extend the invitation to his staff, but Rin had noticed that her father never partook of the frivolities. He usually retreated to his own chamber, as was his normal custom; he was prone to taking hour-long cat naps, snoring louder than the common man while leaving his pillow wet with drool, while other times he wasn't anywhere to be found.

Both extremes annoyed Rin because that meant she was left to entertain herself for countless hours. She had older cousins, who paid her little heed, but she didn't relish being in their company nor the ones who raised them. Her father's stories served as a good reminder that if ever she felt she could trust the king—her uncle— she had countless reasons not to. How could someone she was supposed to love be so heartless?

"I'm a bit brazen, I admit, but a confident personality must match a handsome face," her kingly uncle had once said, defending himself against his brother's attacks.

Rin had tried to cover her laugh; she didn't find him very attractive at all.

Her uncle hadn't *always* been a bad man, but he *wasn't* a good one either. He knew how to love in part, though he loved material things more than people. But despite all his wickedness, he was a devoted husband to his wife and father to his children, and Rin admired that since she didn't have a mother of her own.

His wife often tried to fill the role of mother with an, *"Oh, my dear, but you must wear the green dress with the lower neckline. It'll bring out your eyes and your other* features,*"* before ogling herself in the mirror, plumping her features and disregarding Rin entirely. Sometimes it'd be, *"Don't eat that, darling, or it'll go straight to your thighs. No prince will want you then."* It was soon made evident that she was selfish as well as *vain* and would rather indulge her senses in worldly pleasures than uphold the importance of family.

Quite the pair, those two.

But if Rin knew anything, it was this: as her disdain for the king grew, her adoration for her father increased all the more. And her gratitude for Markhus Roder's undermining of her wicked uncle was her secret pleasure.

Rin didn't approve of his frivolous lifestyle, nor his treatment of those less fortunate than him, and she found his personality unbearable. She liked to think that her father's frequent absences were slight forms of rebellion against his brother's leadership, and she loved him all the more for it. Though she did question where he always ran off to.

If he wasn't in the castle, where was he?

And was he currently wondering the same about her?

Rin swallowed at the thought, focusing instead on pleasanter things. Being up high in the evergreens, a world completely unknown to her, brought a newfound sense of freedom; however, what was coming would be anything but freeing—or so she thought. She heard footsteps in the far-off distance, but since she was uncertain of their number or their course, the cadence only heightened her anxiety. Her palms were slick with sweat, and a droplet on her brow slid down her temple.

She had stolen her father's small dagger in case she needed it, but Rin wasn't sure she'd be confident enough to use it. Still, holding it gave her a sense of power. And, whether her uncle's Royal Guard had tracked her down or it was some other danger, she wanted to be prepared regardless.

Rin's green eyes peered through the dense foliage in front of her, darting to the left and right. She couldn't recall being seen before she fled from home, but her uncle had eyes everywhere. He paid them to be that way, and she couldn't help but feel as though they would be on her trail in a matter of minutes—if they weren't already. Perhaps it would be her father coming for her instead. She wasn't sure what would be worse.

But the footsteps began to trail off in the distance. Overpowered by the sweet melodies of meadowlarks chirping on the branches above her, Rin's heart began to steady itself as she replaced the dagger.

Something caught her eye.

The sun, still penetrating the forest canopy, made its way to the grassy earth. Light fragments touched everything visible, but something in particular shone on the ground.

Curiosity besting caution, she slowly made her descent to the forest floor. The crackling of leaves and twigs met her suede moccasins as she let them take her full weight. Walking over to the glimmering object, its form began to take clearer shape with each forward footstep. A golden coin.

How interesting. Rin bent to pick it up, and she held it to the light and stared. The intricate marking of a hawk was as familiar as the lines on her palm. Without thinking, Rin reached into her own pocket and drew out its exact match, the one her father gave her when she was only a young girl. "It's one and the same!"

It had been years since she last heard one of her father's stories of the rebellion and Markhus Roder's call for justice, but seeing the two coins together made it feel like it'd just been yesterday.

Gooseflesh rising, adrenaline flooding her veins, Rin stood up quickly, unaware that something had caught on her foot. She took a step to the left and landed squarely on her rear before the rest of her body was yanked skyward.

Her breath was knocked from her lungs as a rope burn tore at her ankle. The dagger fell from its sheath and landed on the ground, along with the two coins she'd been holding.

Panic seized her throat as blood rushed to her head.

"Somebody help! Help!" Rin tried to loosen the grip of the rope while hoping to get the attention of a passerby or, better yet, her father. She knew she'd be in trouble, but she didn't care anymore; she just wanted to be freed.

But would he even be in the Everwood? He kept to himself and disappeared often, so why would he come here? Maybe she should have stayed inside like he said; there were too many dangers that lurked about in these woods.

"Please…" She began her cry for help once more but stopped short when something flew past her head and alighted in the trees above her. She craned her neck and squinted her eyes, just barely making out the shape of some sort of bird resting on a branch. Another sound brought her attention lower, and she saw a figure cloaked in midnight black slinking through the forest. Her heart was in her throat. *Please don't hurt me!*

Gentle footsteps made their way over to her hanging body, and she was able to catch a better glimpse of her perpetrator—or rescuer.

"It looks like you fell into the wrong trap, lass," he said. "This was meant for burglars, you know. Those too greedy to pass up a lone coin."

Rin gaped, too shocked to speak. The black cloak, the black gloves that fitted his hands ever so perfectly, the hawk, and the coin… She couldn't see his face, but she didn't have to in order to guess who this could be.

Hope flared in her chest. "Markhus Roder?" she finally sputtered. "Is it really you?"

"That's what they call me."

"I half feared you were only a legend!" Rin smiled in spite of her current predicament. She was impossibly lightheaded, but her heart had never felt so hopeful.

"Legend? Nay, I'm very real." The man talked with a strange accent, and Rin couldn't tell if it was authentic or not.

Markhus Roder walked to the tree which held Rin hostage and cut loose the rope, making sure to catch her falling body in the process. Once she was in his arms, he gently placed her on her feet. Then he bent to pick up her dagger. "Yours, I presume?"

My father's. She nodded.

He handed her the weapon along with the two coins.

"Thank you," she said. Rin had so many questions just waiting to spill out, but Markhus spoke again before she could.

"What is a girl your age doing out here alone in Irindel's Bluff, in the infamous Everwood? It isn't safe," he said curtly.

Rin shifted on her feet. "I'm from the castle. My…my father forbade me to leave the grounds, but I couldn't bear it any longer. I hate feeling like some caged bird." It was puzzling how easily the truth came out to this stranger, but she felt as though she'd known him most of her life through her father's tales.

"You feel caged? It's unsafe in these parts because the Royal Guard are idiots. The king is strict, and he has eyes everywhere. The system is corrupt. Any attempt at helping the poor renders one imprisoned or worse. Haven't you been taught that?" His tone was still gruff, but it was tempered now with compassion.

"Yes, but I don't care," Rin said, lifting her chin. "I want to be like you, helping the poor and standing up for what's right. Why can't my father see that?" And to herself, she mumbled, "Maybe he still blames me for my mother's death." She looked down, rubbing her thumb over the hawks engraved in the coins' metal.

"Blames you?" Apparently, Markhus Roder had heard her. "Surely not! That doesn't seem like the fatherly thing to do. Perhaps he was just trying to protect you from the truth… That maybe your mother died by other means…" Markhus' voice trailed off as if wishing he could recall the words back, but something in his tone made Rin wonder.

"Markhus Roder, do you know something I don't?" she asked, her brow pinched.

He shifted his stance. "I'm not sure what you mean."

Rin took half a step forward, attempting to search his hidden gaze. Was he lying? But what need would a stranger have to lie to her for? Though she knew him from the stories, he owed her nothing. She sighed. "I guess it was just wishful thinking." She looked down at the coins in her hands again, wondering where her father was and what he would say if he saw her here with the infamous cloaked vigilante.

Maybe she should go home, turn around and walk back through

this forest. She'd come here to escape, but so far, she was just more confused. And disappointed. She didn't know what she'd hoped to find in the Everwood, but it wasn't to get lectured by Markus Roder; she got enough of that in Hawksbrooke.

"I should probably get going." Rin took a step back, eyeing Fidget in the trees. Would she get reprimanded upon walking through the castle gates?

She was about to turn around and find out, but she didn't get very far.

Markhus Roder cleared his throat, stopping her mid-spin. "I knew your mother," he finally said.

He knew my mother? The words were like a balm to her heart. Markhus Roder, the helper of the poor, the fighter of the wrongs against Sherwoode Village, knew her mother.

"You did?" Hope once again blossomed in her chest. "Can you tell me about her? My father refuses to."

There was a long pause. "I'll tell you what I know. She was a beautiful woman, much like yourself, with a fiery spirit and green eyes. She had a deep passion for helping those less fortunate. She loved so well." Markhus Roder's voice cracked, but only briefly before he continued. "But that very passion is what got her killed."

"Killed? By whom? She didn't die giving birth to me?" Rin's eyes stung with this knowledge; was her entire existence a farce? "Why would my father lie about something like that?"

"Because maybe he wanted to protect you. If you found out the truth about your mother, maybe he thought you'd want to risk your life doing the same thing. He couldn't fathom that. But your mother was so headstrong with a streak of integrity like the world had never seen. Nothing could stop her from doing the right thing…only death itself." Markhus wasn't looking at her but hurt and sorrow laced his every word.

"What happened?" Rin's heart hammered against her ribs. She was almost afraid of the answer. Could she handle the truth?

"I wasn't there. I was told she went into town disguised as a beggar with food hidden in her garments. And as she was feeding the poor, she found herself in the midst of a street fight; some thugs were harassing produce vendors, and your mother got caught in the fray." He paused to steady his voice. "As she tried to escape, the Royal Guard showed up, arresting everyone, even the poor who weren't involved. Your mother tried pleading on their behalf; one of the guards took one look at her and realized she was a proper woman, not some beggar, and that she had been giving out food. Before anyone had a chance to stop him, she was tried and hanged that very day." Markhus brushed at his eyes, and Rin didn't realize she was crying herself until tears trickled onto her collarbone.

"My uncle killed my mother?" The words tasted of poison as they left her mouth; how could he? Sure, it was his men, but couldn't he have stopped them? Rin tried swallowing the growing lump in her throat, barely choking out the words. "How old…how old was I?" She needed to know, though it wasn't likely Markhus Roder would have a clue.

"Only seven months," he said without hesitation.

So young. "Where was my father during all of this? Why didn't he save her?" A wave of anger flared in her stomach.

"Your father had been away on business for a few days, sent by the king himself. When he came home, he found his wife missing and an updated execution list nailed to the chapel door. The king hadn't known at the time that it was his brother's wife his men had killed, but he soon found out, and it grieved him greatly. The entire kingdom mourned for months..."

"How could they not have known it was my mother? Are they blind?" Rin's voice rose in pitch.

"I can only guess at this. Your mother refused to state her claim; she wanted to die valiantly, as someone who stood her ground and didn't bend to the jurisdiction of an unjust rule."

"How do you know all of this? How do I know you're telling me the truth?" She'd been fed lies all her life; what if these were only more?

But instead of responding, Markhus Roder glanced upward ever so slightly, as if trying to settle on something, revealing a pair of brown eyes and a few strands of auburn hair that protruded from underneath his hood. And, after a decided moment, two gloved hands reached up to remove the head covering, revealing a familiar broken-and-tear-streaked face.

In his eyes, Rin saw the hurt and the truth, the aching and the longing.

"Father?" She spoke through her own tears. Her heart cracked and splintered along with his. *He's Markhus Roder?* None of this made sense, and yet all of it did. The stories. The disappearances. The fake accent. "Why didn't you say something?" she asked, uncertain if she should be thrilled or upset. This was all so much to take in.

"I wanted to tell you, Rinnie. I really did. But I felt powerless."

"Powerless?" She sniffled, incredulous.

He nodded. "Your mother's death was more than I could bear. And seeing you looking so much like her yourself, I wanted to protect you." He reached out to grab her gently by the shoulders, and she was too stunned to move. "I loved your mother, and knowing she died standing up for what she believed was right…it wrecked me. And at the hands of my brother's men."

"Why isn't Uncle off his throne? He should be in prison!" Rin balled her hands into fists.

"My brother is cruel and often calloused, but there is still some good in him, Rin. It's buried deep, but it's there. It was an honest mistake; he didn't know your mother was the one he sent to be executed. Believe me, it's taken a while for me to forgive— oftentimes, I'm not even sure I have." Her father ran a hand over his face.

"Honest? You call that honest? What about justice?" Through Rin's anger, there was a burgeoning sorrow.

"Justice will come, but it's not for me to enact. For now, it's the everyday heroes like your mother, like myself, and like you who can only do the best we can. I became Markhus Roder the day after her death. I needed to find a way to fight back, to honor her memory and keep her spirit alive. If I tried to avenge her death with violence—which, believe me, I have contemplated many times— the kingdom would fall, and I'd lose my brother for good. He's not perfect, Rin, but I'm not fit to rule, either—I can't abide royalty as it is. I belong out here," he continued, gesturing to the trees, the Everwood lit by morning sunlight, "fighting for our people this way. Giving back their voices and their humanity one act of valor at a time. And as much as your uncle is a gluttonous man, he's not averse to love. I just pray that in time he changes his ways for good."

Rin felt like she was seeing her parents anew. Her mother: a true hero, a fighter of the good, and an upholder of all that is right; a woman of strength and fortitude who didn't back down even when death stared her in the face. And her father: a broken and hurt man with a heart as golden as the shining sun. To forgive someone for his wife's death, let alone it being his own brother. To be spurred on by injustice in order to create justice itself in the form of Markhus Roder, the man who stole from the rich to give to the poor. A man who loved and protected fiercely. A man who understood how to give and how to take but knew it was beyond his power to do anything more. *That* was her father.

"I don't know how I can know this information and ever be the same again. How can I return to that castle knowing my own uncle was responsible for my mother's death?" Tears clung to her lashes.

"You learn to fight back." He said it so confidently Rin almost wanted to laugh. But she quickly stifled it once her father's expression grew serious. He pulled a longbow and a quiver out from beneath his cloak and placed them in her hands. "Not in violence, but in defense. Cunning. I'll teach you."

"You're going to let me leave the castle? Freely?" Rin stared in wonder.

"You broke your promise, and I lied to you. We both have made mistakes, but none so grave as the wrongs committed against your mother. None so grave as the crimes against our people. Yes, Rin, I believe you're ready."

Rin grasped the weapons in her hands like they were relics. Finally, she'd be able to leave the castle grounds whenever she wanted, and finally she'd be able to make some changes. She was free. She accepted the gifts wholeheartedly.

She strapped the quiver to her back and slung the bow over her shoulder like she'd seen her father do so many times. She was only too ready to be following in the footsteps of her parents. But a weight still pressed on her heart, one that felt like a resurfaced wound mixed with the rawness of a new cut.

She was willing to fight back—wanted to, even. There was this burning need to uphold the truth and see good deeds done.

If only forgiveness would come as willingly.

Suddenly, her father whistled through his teeth, and Fidget, the hawk, flew from his perch and circled the air.

But instead of settling on Markhus Roder's shoulder, he alighted upon Rin's. His talons were sharp, but they didn't puncture her clothing; they only rested there as a steady reminder that he was wild and bred for the hunt. He was dangerous, yes, but he knew better than to attack a prey larger than himself.

She felt a sudden kindredness with the hawk. She was no longer caged; she was free. And though her joy was bound with grief— sunshine and sharp talons—she looked once more to her father, whose spirit was both broken and radiant like the morning.

It would take time, she was more than certain. She loathed her uncle, couldn't stand to be related to him, but if her parents sought goodness through acts of valor and kindness, she'd follow in their footsteps. Resorting to anger never solved anything, hence what happened to her mother.

She was determined to fight for forgiveness just as much as for what was right.

Sunshine and talons. Joy and grief. Perhaps life was a mixture of the two.

"Ready to go home, Rin?" her father asked.

She looked once more at the Everwood, taking in its tall evergreens and pines, breathing in the scent of sap and the outdoors. These woods had grown her as much as the stories she'd grown up hearing. She hated to leave so soon, but she was too weary to do much after all she had just learned.

"Tomorrow? Can we come back here then?"

Her father smiled. "We can. I'm sure Fidget would like that. But tonight, how about another story?"

She smiled, too, in spite of her heavy heart. "I'd like that."

The Everwood and the journey toward forgiveness could wait until morning.

The End

Storm-Crow

(A *Robin Hood* retelling)

The daily maritime bell rings its deep, metallic song, signaling the hour to pack up and go home. Its chime rivals the midnight-colored birds cawing in the skies, circling the harbor below.

"Thief at large. Beware the Storm-Crow! Guard your catches; secure your traps!" A man yells at the corner of the bay, his booted feet planted firmly on the wooden boards of the wharf, a gloved hand cupped around his mouth and his other ringing the bell.

Everyone listens and scurries along, fishermen locking up their booths and securing their catches in ice buckets before trudging home for the night. Their eyes stray warily to the sky as if afraid one of the birds might swoop low and ravage the fish.

The same proclamation resounds throughout the docks every day, traveling up the cobblestone streets, through the doors of seaside homes, and invited to stay for dinner. It's all anyone talks about. The biggest news in Harborside—a port town that really isn't known for much aside from its fish.

Doors lock prematurely, as do the windows. Fish markets close early and are patrolled by officers every other hour. And when the day is done, the gossipers take to the streets and spill their newfound rumors.

"I heard a mackerel vanished off Lloyd's stand this afternoon. And a carp to boot!" An elderly lady throws her hands in the air, nearly casting off her faux muff in the process.

"That's not all, Lotte; did you hear about Felix? One minute there were five tuna on his boat, and then the next, they were gone! Poof! Just like that! Some folks say they flopped back into the water, but Felix doesn't think so. 'Rightly caught, they were. Rightly caught an' half dead,' he said. I'd bet my last two cents it was the Storm-Crow's doing. He's just like these darn Harborside crows, waiting for others to do the work and then stealing the plunder from right under their noses. Scavengers, all of them!" The second elderly lady draws the folds of her coat closer to her chin, shivering.

"One thing's for sure, Margueritte. If we don't get inside soon, this chill will become a thief too, stealing more of our warmth than is proper. The time for afternoon walks has reached its end, I'm afraid. Winter's nearly upon us."

The two women lean into the biting winds and proceed up the street, huddled together, walking toward their weather-beaten homes. All of Harborside's houses are variations of blues and greens, as if the ocean had extended its hand and bestowed some of the port town with its personality. The women pass a stretch of run-down tackle shacks to their left, missing the figure lurking in the shadows.

A cloaked man peels his body from the cedar wall and tugs his hood farther over his eyes.

Storm-Crow. He never grows tired of hearing that.

He draws open the folds of his thick cloak and readjusts the burlap sack beneath. The faint smell of fish dances just under his nose before the wind takes the scent away.

"The perfume of victory," he whispers to himself, breaking out of the shadows and taking his place on the narrow street.

The bitter winds pull at his cloak and sting his wrists. He tugs on his gloves, trying to shield any parts of his bare skin. Aside from the face, a man is most recognizable by his hands. The hands reveal a lot about one's character: his line of work, his hours of labor, and even his opinion of himself.

In short, a man can't afford to get caught when so much depends on his hands remaining hidden.

The man hunches his back and proceeds on his normal route through the sights and sounds of Harborside. Up the street, past the blue-green cottages of the elite, and finally into the rougher part of the village where the poor live and everything is overgrown and brown. The bungalows barely stand upright, as if the subtlest breath of wind will blow them over. Most houses are simply tarps or huts made of driftwood—gifts from the sea.

He steps to the nearest shanty and rifles through his pack.

Grabbing a tail, he pulls out the mackerel, scaly and slimy in the waning daylight, and places the fish on the doormat, knocking lightly on the door before running away. He moves to the next shack and does the same thing until every home is supplied.

When the moon breaks through the amassing clouds, the man knows his job is finished for the night.

He sighs in relief.

Tomorrow, he'll begin all over again.

***

The maritime bell rings loudly, and even in his groggy state, the man realizes he's overslept. He groans and grabs his thick overcoat before crawling out from under an upturned red boat. It isn't every night he sleeps in his hideout, but when the trek home seems too long, roughing it out in the old shipyard isn't too bad an option. It just means he wakes up with a sore back and strained neck muscles; he only hopes his boss won't fire him on the spot and make matters worse.

Stealing fish is a lot harder if he's unemployed.

He books it to the docks, taking once more to the cobblestone streets, and accidentally bumps his shoulder into a stocky man standing near the water's edge.

"Eyy, watch it." The man shoves him sideways, his eyes dawning in sudden realization. "Finnick. You're late. Capt'n ain't too 'appy."

Finnick nods and pulls at his collar before walking toward the *Barbet*, a ship named after some green, exotic bird in the south.

He'd do well not to rub shoulders with Horace again. The man is as wild as a tidal wave.

Finnick takes hold of the rigging and swings his body forward before landing with a light thump on the deck. All his years as a thief have cautioned him to be feather-footed.

"Took ye long enough, eh?" The sound of his boss's irritated voice rises above the seawinds.

Not feather-footed enough.

The captain stalks forward, his forehead dotted with sweat despite the chilly air.

"Overslept." Finnick shrugs and grabs a mass of fishing line by his feet, untangling the impossible fibers. His hand catches on a loose barb, his knuckles sliced open in the shape of a crooked 'S.'

He bites back a grimace, the wound stinging in the salty wind. *Brilliant.*

"Not worth yer time, mate. Gus's already set the lines on the port an' starboard. As for ye, I'd like ye to come with me."

Finnick's heart beats twice as fast. *This can't be good.*

He follows his boss to the stern and enters the captain's cabin. Though his boss is just a common seaman with no official licensure, he goes by *captain* on board. Captain Ambros, that is. It's a bit excessive, but with the *Barbet* being a commandeered pirate ship and its crew just as salty, the title fits.

"Sit." Captain Ambros gestures to a rugged stool and crosses the room to look out the back window. He eyes the lifeboat hanging beyond the glass, the only one this vessel boasts, strategically placed for the captain and the captain alone. He pauses long, but the continuous opening and closing of his mouth tells Finnick he's trying to speak. Finally, he clears his throat. "You've 'eard the rumors?"

Finnick shifts in his seat. "Rumors, Capt'n?" Something tells him he knows where this conversation is headed.

"Ol' Lloyd and Felix be swindled again. Cheated right out o' their purses," he says, and Finnick does everything he can not to roll his eyes. They are the two wealthiest fishmongers on this side of the harbor; they can afford to lose a few pennies or five. "An' I believe I know just who done it." The captain turns and levels Finnick with his piercing gaze.

Finnick's hands twitch on his lap. *Me? But I am so careful. I move under the cover of darkness; the night is my cloak.* He swallows the lump in his throat. "Capt'n?"

"Listen, Finnick. I didn't hire an addlebrained landlubber for nothin'. I hired ye to secure ol' *Barby* 'ere. More 'ands on deck means less opper'tunies for thievin' ones." The captain walks from the window and takes a seat across from him. "But somethin' tells me this Storm-Crow of ours be settin' his sights on ol' *Barby-girl* tonight."

Finnick lets out a discrete sigh. *So he doesn't suspect me.* "Capt'n?" Finnick twitches again.

"Blast, Finnick!" The man slams his fist down on the table in front of him. "Can't ye say anythin' more than 'Capt'n?' Ye as bloody annoying as Gus's parrot."

Finnick's nerves grow fuzzy. Normally he's not this jumpy, but he's been upping the stakes as of late, and now it seems even his boss is growing suspicious.

"What makes you think that" —he pauses, clearing his throat—

"the Storm-Crow will come here tonight?" It feels odd saying his own epithet, but if the captain thinks he can guess Finnick's game, he'll have to think again.

"'Cause I'm keepin' some fresh catches on me ship. Unlocked. Ready for the takin'. A thief can't resist what's easy. But I bet ye he tries the locks an' picks up just the same, no matter the night."

Finnick swallows, feeling as if his methods have been exposed, his lock-picking tools weighing heavy in his pocket. But he shrugs it off, suddenly emboldened with an idea. "And how will you apprehend him?"

"Easy. While the Storm-Crow catches whiff of ol' *Barby* whilst doin' his usual route, he'll climb aboard an' search her. The fish will be in this very room."

"And where will you be?"

"Hiding, o' course. Behind that door." He points to the single exit to the outside world. "When our thief enters this chamber, I'll trap 'im inside and make him wish he'd never been born."

Finnick purses his lips. "You're certain of this? That the Storm-Crow will come?"

"I swear it on me own mother's grave. Ye know why they call him Storm-Crow, Finnick?"

He'd heard the tales plenty of times, could practically sing them in his sleep, but something compels him to shake his head, inviting the captain to divulge his tale.

Captain Ambros sighs. "Ye thicker than the broadside of a whale, mate." He smirks, plastering on a conniving grin. "They call him Storm-Crow 'cause his coming be like an approaching gale, often predictable with the patterns in the weather. 'Red sky in morning, sailors take warning. Red sky at night, sailor's delight,' an' all that lot. But in his case, fish in the market means fish in his pocket. He comes like a storm—wherever he catches the scent— and like a crow descending on carrion that isn't his own, he takes what isn't his, ye see?"

Finnick nods, amused at this elaborate exposition of his secret moniker.

"He'll be 'ere tonight, and if he don't show up, he's a bigger fool than me thought." The captain chuckles and fixes his gaze on Finnick once more. "I'd like ye to keep watch with me."

"Me?" Finnick rubs a hand along the back of his neck, suppressing the urge to laugh—or cringe. *This makes matters rather…delicate.* "What for?"

"When I catch the blasted criminal, ye'll 'ave ta bind his feet. Can't do it all meself, I'm afraid."

"What of Horace? Gus? Couldn't they help you?" Finnick asks.

Captain Ambros crosses his arms. "I don't want those snots. I want *ye*. Unless…" He narrows his eyes. "There's a reason ye can't be here."

Finnick tenses and tries to keep his expression placid. "I'll come."

"Splendid!" The captain claps his hands, standing up and making for the door. "Report back 'ere by seven. I've a good feelin' 'bout tonight. A night ta remember." He chuckles and twists the knob before he pauses and glances over his shoulder. "Oh, and Finnick—nasty business, those barbs. By the looks of it, one got ye good." Captain Ambros runs his gaze along Finnick's knuckles, shaking his head with wry humor. "Best not bleed yerself dry, mate.

Ye know where the bandages are." He walks outside into the cold night air.

Finnick takes his shirt and swipes at the blood dripping over his fingers. The cuts aren't deep, but they won't stop bleeding.

A night ta remember.

"I guess that's one way to put it." Finnick expels a half-hearted breath, wondering how on earth he's going to pull something like this off.

***

The fog rolls in, and it's nearing seven o'clock. Finnick adjusts his pack and makes for the docks again. As he nears, the same telltale crows caw above him, their flying forms darker shadows amidst an already darkened sky.

The feathered beasts are his namesake.

Something like pride washes over him. And then guilt pricks his conscience. Crows take what isn't theirs as a means of survival; they steal and scavenge, but can they be blamed when it's built into their design? Finnick, on the other hand… He knows his actions are punishable by Harborside's standards, but what of the poor? Crows take for themselves, but Finnick—he takes on behalf of others. To feed those who haven't an extra penny to spare.

He could go fishing, had even borrowed a boat on numerous occasions, but time was short and people were hungry. Not even the coins that line his pockets are enough to feed them all. It's always easier to take what is already caught.

Like the crows do.

Though he is always cautious to only take from those who can afford it, like Lloyd and Felix and even his boss, Ambros, who hold a monopoly over the port.

He doesn't have to take the bait and steal the fish tonight, but how can he let this opportunity go to waste? Too many families rely on Finnick's support. And he won't let them down now.

With renewed confidence, he looks up and squints at the squawking shadows. *Tonight.* "The night of the Storm-Crow," he whispers.

Finally, when he steps onto the *Barbet,* his racing mind slows. He knows what he has to do. Tucking his belongings behind a barrel, he proceeds to the captain's cabin, whistling.

"Finnick, that you?" the captain calls.

"Aye."

"Good, good. Come in an' take a looksie at the plunder."

Finnick steps over the threshold and is assaulted by the scent of the sea. A pile of fish lay on the table in the center of the room, the smell intoxicating.

Confined quarters sure makes the job a lot smellier.

"Nice what you've done with the place," Finnick remarks.

"Don't be cheeky, mate. Tis' just the start. We'll be settin' all Harborside free with our act o' charity tonight. I'd bet my golden tooth on it." The captain moves to his position behind the door. "Best hide, too. Behind the tackle boxes there." He points at the desired location.

Finnick does as he's told, and the minutes tick by in an endless stream of silence. He looks at the clock hanging above the doorway; it's nearing eight.

Almost time.

"Captain?" Finnick whispers in the dark.

He hears shuffling and then a mumbled reply. "What?"

"Tank's full. Gotta take a leak."

"Now, Finnick? Of all the blasted…" The captain mutters a string of curse words. He sighs. "Fine. But make it quick."

Oh, I will.

Finnick maneuvers through the dark and exits the captain's quarters, walking the deck to find his bag. He strips his outer coat and switches it for the cloak inside, rummaging through the folds of fabric for his gloves. His heart rate speeds up. *No. No. No. Where are they?* It's a pointless search no matter how many times he rifles through the contents.

No gloves. How could he have forgotten his gloves?

He shoves down his worries, surveying his appearance. He is unrecognizable from head to toe; his hands won't betray him. Not if he plays his cards right.

He shoves the bag aside and grabs an empty one, tucking it through the belt around his waist. He takes one of the nearby barrels and tosses it over the edge of the ship, waiting for the telltale splash to echo loudly over the natural turn of the waves.

"Step one," Finnick says.

He draws his hood and makes for the captain's cabin. At the door, he turns the knob and pushes the door in. But instead of entering the room, he takes a step back and retreats further into the shadows outside.

A few minutes roll by, drenched in silence. Finally, Finnick hears something like a strangled cough or faint whisper in the dark.

"Finnick?" Silence. "Finnick? Is that you?"

Finnick remains quiet, waiting for the perfect moment.

Footsteps echo in the darkness, tentatively stepping over the threshold and onto the deck. "Finnick?" the captain calls again, softer this time. He walks a few more steps beneath the moonlight.

Finnick moves behind him like a shadow and slips into the captain's quarters undetected, closing and locking the door in the process.

"Step two."

A few paces into the room and a sharp cry pierces the night air. Heavy fists pound on the door. "Open up! Open up, ye scabby sea bass!" Captain Ambros shouts.

Finnick takes out the empty bag lashed around his waist and fills it with the fish. The stench is pungent, but his hands work fast.

Suddenly, the door behind him splinters, and the captain kicks the rest of it in. He stands in the doorway, a short pike in his hand, brandished and at the ready. "I knew I'd find ye in here, ye filthy bilge-sucking barnacle."

"Nice one. Is that original?" Finnick disguises his voice, side-stepping around the table and slinging his stolen goods over his shoulder with satisfaction. Many hungry stomachs will be fed tonight.

"Ye hornswoggle!" The captain's nostrils flare.

"Tsk, tsk. Such language." Finnick shakes his head.

"Just hand over the bloody fish!" The captain inches closer, his face set in a grimace.

"Or what?"

"I heard what ye did. Ye tossed me man Finnick overboard. I'll 'ave ye hanged for ye crimes once tonight be through. Ye 'ave blood on ye 'ands along with the scent o' stolen goods." The captain spits across the table, and the projectile lands on the front of Finnick's cloak.

Finnick wipes at it, stilling instantly as the moonlight streaming in through the window illuminates his still-bloody knuckles.

He'd taken his bandage off a few hours ago to allow the wound to air out. And now he'd wished he'd kept it on.

Blast.

It's enough to capture Captain Ambros' attention. His gaze lingers on the *S*-shaped cut, and his scowl turns into one of confusion as he lowers his pike an inch. "Ye 'ave actual blood on ye 'ands." His brows pucker together as something washes over him. "Strange marking… coincidental, even."

Finnick fights to maintain his nerve. "A paring knife. Devilish little things, really."

"Curious. Never seen a paring knife make that type o' scar in me life." The captain shifts his pike lower. "Looks more like…" He pauses and lunges for Finnick's hood.

Barnacles.

Finnick ducks before running to the back window. He flings open the glass, but not soon enough. Captain Ambros' hand lands on his shoulder, yanking him backward and holding fast to his cloak. "Got ye now, ye sleazy bottom-dweller," he says.

Finnick's heart might as well be a hummingbird's wings. With one hand, he fumbles with the knot at his neck and discards his disguise, launching his body and the bag of fish into the cool of the night. He lands heavily in the lifeboat beyond and lets loose the rigging before the captain has a chance at stopping his retreat.

The boat descends at a rapid pace before smacking the water with a terrific slap, the bow dipping forward and nearly filling up in the process. Finnick steadies the vessel and grabs the oars, plunging them into the murky blue, heaving with all his might.

"I know it's ye, Finnick! Storm-Crow!" Captain Ambros yells, holding up his cloak. "Yer a dead man! An' dead men tell no tales!"

Finnick ignores him. His cover may have been blown, but he still has the fish. That's why he took the job in the first place—to be closer to his catch. He'll just find another port to plunder before staking his claim on Harborside once again.

It might make the trek more difficult, but it doesn't matter. He'll do anything to keep the poor in his neighborhood from going hungry.

Some might call him a villain, but to them, he's a hero. It makes being on the run worth it.

Maybe Storm-Crow will pillage Seaport. After all, he's heard they're in the market for a good thief, and where there's a storm, a crow is sure to follow.

The End

Moral of the story (especially if reading with children):
Stealing should neither be glorified nor encouraged, but much like the infamous Robin Hood, he chose to do what was right on behalf of those who had less than him. Instead of turning toward the route of crime, perhaps think outside the box on how you can better serve those around you. And maybe, just maybe, you might find yourself whisked away on a grand adventure.

Like Stars in the Sky

(A *Peter Pan* inspired tale)

*"Don't be afraid to grow up, Pete my boy, but stay curious.
Always stay curious. The stories keep us young."*

Part One

~

Pete

I can't do this anymore, Pete." A watch lands on the cobblestone pavers, its glass face splintering near my shoes. I bend to pick up the discarded gift, turning it over to see my initials carved into its metal underside. *P.J.P. Peter James Parrel.* "We're done."

Done?

"This just isn't working out. You and I *both* know this isn't working out."

"What did I do wrong this time?" I straighten and cross my arms over my chest. I've grown used to these sorts of outbursts by now, most conversations revolving around how regularly I fall short as a boyfriend.

"You're a dreamer, Pete. I want someone whose head isn't always in the clouds." She throws her hands up in the air as if to prove her point. "I need someone to *ground* me. Not fill my head with nonsense and delusion. We're a lost cause together. *You're* a lost cause. A lost…a lost boy. And I'm over it!"

Ouch.

"Goodbye, Pete." Without even a tear, my girlfriend for the past year turns on her heels and stalks away, disappearing within the throng of people on the bustling streets of London.

I don't think I'll be seeing Beverly Meaver ever again.

As if in agreement, Big Ben chimes his hourly notice. The deep tones reverberate from the tower, finalizing the end of the relationship—like it's etching it into London's history.

"I suppose that's it, then." I stuff my hands into my pockets, the cracked pieces of my watch brushing up against my left thumb. Poets might say this symbolizes the state of my heart, but the muscle can't break—it's just bruised. Tired. Looking for a place to belong.

I pick my way along the cobblestones, kicking up loose gravel as I walk toward the clock tower. People on bicycles speed by me, mothers tote their wily children home, and old men pack up their chess games at the local park. The scent of fresh bread wafts under my nose, and I glance to my right, seeing two young ladies enjoying an early-evening conversation at an outdoor cafe.

On most occasions, I enjoy London, but sometimes… I shove my hands further into my pockets, shaking my head to dispel the memory of Beverly and her crushing words.

I've never been good with women—or rather, none seem to understand me. I just wish I could meet someone like my father did with my mother; they were perfectly suited. He made time for things that mattered to her and vice versa, but above all, he was a great listener. And that's what made him such a good storyteller.

As my mother fixed supper, he would spin endless tales, and it was the night sky which he loved talking about the most. He would always finish with, *"The stars have stories of their own, Pete my boy. Ones truer than many here on earth. You'd do well to learn them,"* while my mother, dinner made, sat at his feet and threaded her fingers through his. Theirs was a happy marriage: warm meals, countless stories, and marveling at the stars.

Hence why I've worked at the Royal Observatory Greenwich ever since I was old enough for a job, filling in my father's role as manager once he passed.

I thought to make the stars my profession, too, hoping to glimpse but a fraction of his wonder.

Because he was right.

The tales of old wove their way into my veins, much like the earth and heavens. Tales such as *King Arthur*, *Robin Hood*, or my favorite—*Peter Pan*.

But instead of these stories, women like Beverly wish my attention was claimed elsewhere. *"There's no room for such foolish tales in a grown man's life,"* they'd all say, preferring I partake in more worthy pursuits. But what can invoke more wonder than the stars aside from the One who created them?

Not *all* women are like this, I know, but all the ones interested in me seem to be…

Bleh. I take my hand out of my pocket and run it through my too-long auburn strands. I don't care. I *shouldn't* care.

I press onward, the din of Big Ben resounding slowly in the airspace above me. When the sun dips low in its late-afternoon descent, my home resides within the clock's long shadow for half an hour. A hovel in the darkness. My retreat.

It's comforting to live within the shadow of something so grand. Magical, even. And when nighttime comes and all traces of shadow have gone abed, it's the faint glow of Ben's face in the darkness which shines like the stars in the sky.

They are my only companions now.

I've charted Orion's course, watching his pursuit of the Pleiades sisters or his chase of Lepus. And then there's Argo Navis, my favorite—the pirate ship of the heavens.

I can just picture her sails billowing against the backdrop of the night. Her rustic masts, the timbers as strong as bones. Her hull a fortified bowl of mahogany, unwilling to bend beneath cannon fire.

I could get lost amongst them.

I scoff at the irony. Does Beverly have to be right?

By the time I reach my doorstep, the chimes have finished their eighth ring. In less than ten minutes, the sun will disappear entirely, and the starry hosts will greet me once again.

I press the latch on the front door and push it open, flicking on the light switch. The room brightens in a warm, golden glow, reflecting off the windowpanes and glass ships-in-bottles lining the shelves. I plug in the strands of lights hanging off my bookshelf and fireplace, the pinpricks of fairy magic adding an extra dose of brilliance.

And just because, I flick off the electric bulb from above and let the fairy lights claim the room entirely. I prefer it this way—the darkness with specks of light, my own kind of celestial sphere. It's here I'll often sit at night, flipping through stories from the bound tomes on my shelves, poring over the pages as if they were my father's own words.

But not yet; there's only five minutes left until the stars poke their heads from beneath their blanket. Reading can wait, but the outside cannot.

I tug on a light jacket and step out onto the balcony. A glance at the sky shows a thin layer of clouds, but I know if I wait just a moment longer, they will disappear and let the little balls of fire show through. So I bide my time, holding my breath.

I scan the expanse, squinting until I can make out the beginnings of Canis Major. And sure enough, after the clouds dissipate altogether, Argo Navis blinks into view, regal in all her majesty.

Once again, I'm transported, but this time, it feels real. For how can one look upon the stars and not hear their stories anew? If I could but reach them, then perhaps I might learn their true names. Are the stars aware they were labeled by us?

Argo Navis winks as if reading my thoughts, her own tale full of secrets. She beckons me toward her. And suddenly the darkened space surrounding each star-point begins to solidify. First comes the hull, then the masts, and then the sails.

I blink, rubbing my eyes. *Am I dreaming?* I pinch my cheek for good measure.

But the image still remains. The ship—for that is what it is— now shimmers in ethereal gold.

I catch my breath, the reality striking me afresh.

They're real. Dad was right. The stories are actually real!

Suddenly, a gust of wind tousles the hair along my neck. I raise my collar, not daring to peel my eyes away from the sky. The gale picks up speed, and the golden ship rotates so the hull is pointed in my direction. And then it moves swiftly, growing brighter and bigger with each moment that passes.

It's coming toward me.

I'm surprised at the calm I feel. I'm eager to see Argo Navis up close, but there's no fear. Only anticipation.

I've dreamt of this day for a long time, never imagining it to be possible as I stood at the pinnacle of the observatory. Always looking through a lens, never touching.

Beverly thought I was crazy. And maybe I am—I haven't ruled that out entirely.

Am I the only one seeing this?

The pirate ship is a few yards away now, and I silently pray that she doesn't run into Big Ben. The ship swerves to the right, skimming the tops of trees and townhomes, and comes to a stop just above my head.

An anchor cascades down its side as if grounding it in the air while a rope ladder is thrown over the port side and tumbles down in front of me. If I stretch my hand out, I can grasp one of the wooden rungs. I look up even farther and notice a curious set of eyes peering over the bulwark.

They're green and lit with a certain fire. Not the kind that burns, but the kind that listens and understands.

"You coming?" she asks. Her voice lilts on the wind like a dance.

"I...uh..." My tongue is stuck to the roof of my mouth.

"Come on, then!" She waves and then points to the ladder.

I take hold of the wooden contraption, placing one hand on a rung and my foot on another. Steadily, I climb, all the while wondering what in the world I'm doing.

I'm climbing a ladder. To a ship made of stars. And there's a girl. A really pretty girl.

But the higher I go, the surer I feel.

It's as if I was destined for this moment.

At the top of the ladder, I pull myself up and over the railing of the floating vessel, landing heavily on the wooden deck. It sways beneath my feet, the sea made of air rather than water. The smell of fog rather than salt.

I scan the ship's perimeter and notice a young man tugging at the rigging while another man reels in the anchor beside him. Then I look skyward to the crow's nest, where a little boy with a spyglass leans against the basket, his gaze set on the horizon. It's not much—a skeleton crew—and there doesn't seem to be a captain.

"Welcome!" the girl says. "My name is Estella."

I meet her gaze, her face heart-shaped and framed by a blonde head of hair. Her smile is filled with excitement and mischief, and there's a sparkle to her skin, almost as if she is made of stardust.

"Hi." I barely manage to speak past the lump in my throat. "My name's Pete." I have so many questions, but to ask any feels as if I'd break this spell and cast it away for good.

"Hello, Pete. You're aboard the *Wendy Bird*, the swiftest and surest vessel in all the skies," she says, arms spread wide. "She flies as if she has wings."

"Not the Argo Navis, then?"

"Argo Navis?" She rubs her chin. "Oh yes. That's what they call it down there." She gestures to the city below us. "Up here, the stars are called by a different name."

"Do all of them have different names?" I ask, eager to learn them all.

"Aye. And the *Wendy Bird* is only the beginning."

Feeling emboldened, I step forward and ask another question. "Do you think you could teach them to me? Their names?"

Another smile splits Estella's face, the sight a perfect half-moon. "I'd be delighted! But first…" She grabs my hand and drags me up the stairs to the quarterdeck, where a large wheel is attached vertically to a wooden post.

I can't help staring at it, and my hands tingle in unexpected anticipation.

"Go for it." She pushes me forward.

"What? Me?" She wants me to steer this thing?

"Every ship needs a captain. You've studied the stars for years, Pete, enough to have the role be yours. And what better vessel to command than one made of them? You'll be like a star in the sky yourself."

Like a star in the sky.

I like the sound of that. But how does she know I've studied the stars?

Maybe it's because she is one?

I hesitate for only a moment before I walk toward the wheel, placing my hands on the spindles. Running my fingers along the smooth grains, I feel another tingle shoot up my arms, but this time, the sensation is made of heat. Of fire. Of starlight.

"Now, think of a wonderful thought," Estella says beside my shoulder, her gaze locked on the horizon before it meets mine. "Any one will do." She waves her arm over the wheel and golden dust falls from her palm, covering the quarterdeck in skeins of gold before it stretches and reaches around the entirety of the ship.

It's as if we're floating in bronze, on a cloud of light. Like we actually are one of the stars in the sky.

And I think…perhaps I really was lost after all. That is, until now.

Because now I'm home.

Suddenly, the *Wendy Bird* jolts forward, and we're zooming toward the nearest constellation.

"First stop—Taurus. Time to tame the fell beast. And learn his true name, of course." Estella laughs, the sound like the tinkling of bells. Her gaze has resumed its roam of the horizon, but the green of her irises glistens like dew drops on a sunny day.

Swaths of night sky rush past my vision as blossoms of gold and twinkling lights break up the darkness.

My breath hitches in my throat. I'm no longer looking through a glass lens. I'm finally touching the stars!

And I've never felt more alive.

Part Two

~

Estella

I've never felt more alive than at this very moment. It's as if I was simply a shell of myself before, and with the wind rushing past me, jostling my hair and making me squint my eyes toward the horizon, I know the truth deeply.

I *am* alive.

Like the stars.

I grip the wheel tightly, using everything in me to keep the speeding ship on course, my muscles unused to the strain. I'm an astronomer, not a captain. But I'm eager to change that.

"Over there, Pete," Estella says, pointing to a cluster of plasma glowing against the backdrop of the night sky. *Taurus.*

I rotate the ship's wheel and realign the *Wendy Bird*, the bow dipping forward ever so slightly. It's strange navigating a ship for the first time, but Estella was right. Maybe I *am* made for this role.

The cluster of stars draws nearer as the *Wendy Bird* races forward at an unnatural clip, not slowing down in the slightest.

My heart hammers in my chest, and my hands begin to feel the individual splinters of wood as they grip the wheel tighter.

How am I going to stop this thing?

"We need to slow down, Pete!" Estella yells, grabbing hold of my arm. "Too fast, and we'll be absorbed by the Nevervoid!"

"The Nevervoid?" Where's that? *What's* that?

In all my years of studying the night sky, I can only imagine she means a black hole. But isn't a magicked ship supposed to be invincible?

I inhale and cut the wheel sharply to the left, causing the port side to swing around and take the brunt of our momentum. The vessel slows, but it's not enough. At this rate, we'll be shooting past Taurus.

I look skyward and notice the sails oscillating in the wind, like a lung breathing in and out before they pull taut once more, the air filling their canvas bodies.

"We need to take in the sails!" I don't know what compels me to say it, but it feels like the right move.

Estella nods encouragingly as if she was thinking the same thing. "Aye. You're brilliant, Pete!"

She leans over the quarterdeck's railing and hollers to the crew below. In a matter of minutes, the two men have the sails hoisted and strapped in place, and at once, the speed of the *Wendy Bird* finally slows.

The small lad from the crow's nest emerges from his hiding

place, standing on shaky legs. He brings his spyglass clumsily to his eye. "Stardust ahoy! We've made it to Taurus!" he shouts.

Estella looks at me, wonder in her bright eyes. "I knew you'd be a good captain."

I feel my cheeks heat. I don't know what to say; it feels too high of praise for one such as myself. For one so new at this. Especially when we'd been heading toward a black hole.

"That was a close call!" she says, shuddering as if reading my thoughts. Then she points in the direction of Taurus.

The constellation is just beginning to take his shape into a bull—horns shimmering in the moonlight and hooves kicking up stardust. In a few moments, I'll be learning the constellation's true name.

But I'm more interested in what lies beyond him, in the darkened expanse where only two small stars shimmer dully.

"Is that the Nevervoid?" I remember her fear a few minutes ago, her desperation to bypass it at all costs. I walk to the railing and lean against the wooden frame, squinting into the night.

"Aye."

"What is it?" I ask.

Estella joins my side, her shoulder lightly brushing against mine. "The home of dreams. Most of them lost."

"Home? You mean…it's not a black hole?" I glance at her profile, her emerald gaze fixed straight ahead. She looks pensive, as if troubled by some deep thought.

"Not a black hole, no."

"A star then?" I ask, hopeful. Maybe I'll learn its true name, too.

She shakes her head. "It's a place where dreams go and remain ever as they are, never changing or growing, just…forgotten." She seems almost sad.

A long stretch of silence dances between us, bringing us closer and apart with every lingering breath. Who will speak next?

"It's best to stay away." Estella's voice shakes, breaking the stillness. But something in her tone hints that she doesn't quite believe her own words.

I hesitate a moment, my curiosity too great. "What makes you say that?"

My question is met with further silence, as deep and somber as a starless night. She swallows, a shininess glistening in the corners of her eyes. "It was my home."

Was? A weight shifts in my chest, settling in my middle. Guilt prickles my nerves, and I feel its effects trail throughout my body. I don't have it in me to ask further questions. I can't bear to hurt her any more.

"I was born in London," she says suddenly, looking at me. "Much like you, I'd imagine."

I nod, afraid my words will somehow break the spell between us.

"I was brought to the Nevervoid when I was eighteen. My father took me once my mother passed, and it was there where I lived for the past thirty years." She pauses, biting her lip as if waiting for the numbers to compute.

Thirty years? I swallow the lump in my throat. But that would mean… Her youthful face and bright eyes say otherwise. Estella can't be *that* old, can she?

"That's when the trouble started," she adds.

"Trouble?" I choose to vocalize that question instead.

"Aye. My father—he loved the stars, had somehow known there were portals to distant lands beyond shrouds of cloud-cover. He studied the heavens, much like you, Pete. But his study grew treacherous.

"He became obsessed with wealth and immortality, realizing quickly there was something in the air in the Nevervoid, something in its very fibers, which could grant him his deepest wishes." She shakes her head. "The very things which brought his demise. For you see, in the Nevervoid, one never ages. Thus, one wish granted."

An ageless void? I can hardly believe what I'm hearing, yet I know every word she speaks is true, or else why say it at all? "What about the wealth?" Her story pulls me in as if I'm listening to one of my father's riddles, eager to make heads or tails of everything.

"A passing ship, another one made of stardust, somehow got caught in the Nevervoid. It entered the atmosphere out of control and crash-landed on the island. The ship broke apart, scattering coins and treasure everywhere, and within a few days, my father found the wealth had doubled, tripled into the likeness of towering, golden trees." She pauses and takes a breath. "Since then, he's become a pillager of goods, stealing treasure from other passersby and commandeering their ships to add to his pointless fleet. No one would dream to come up against the likes of Jasper Hook. Thus, he'd gotten his second wish."

"How did you get away?"

"I claimed my magic and learned how to fly. Stardust isn't just used for casting light, Pete, but for giving you wings. After thirty ageless years in the Nevervoid, I finally fled my father's greedy ways and sought the Argo Navis, acquiring this ship before he had a chance at taking it for himself."

My head feels like it's about to burst.

Estella seems to notice and steadies me with her hand despite her own sorrow. "Time moves swiftly in the Nevervoid. The years blend together faster than they do on earth. Thirty years has only felt like ten, but even so, that's much too long to remain locked away. I've been free for a few months, Pete. Though the Nevervoid might say otherwise, I've only just turned nineteen."

Her words work like magic, assuring me I'm not losing my mind. Or perhaps I am. But just knowing Estella isn't pushing fifty settles that nagging feeling in my gut. It is all making sense, though this tale sounds crazier by the second.

Here is this girl, *blessedly* only five years my junior, cast in starlight as if she is a star herself, living as a stowaway on board the heavens' surest vessel. She is radiant even in her sorrow, her eyes beacons of hope amidst a past filled with pain.

She clears her throat. "I don't know if I can ever go back—ever face my father again. He's too changed. Too far gone. But I like to think that maybe there's still hope for him to be who he once was. It's a version I sorely miss." She brushes a hand under one of her eyes, taking a deep breath.

"I'm sorry, Estella." I don't know what other words to say. Everything else feels too contrived, out of place, or forced. How do you pick up the pieces of a broken life?

"It's okay. Thanks for listening. I haven't had a chance to talk about this in a while." She glances at the rest of the crew on deck, watching as they interact with Taurus, the bull whose nostrils send puffs of steam into the cool night.

"What about them?" I ask. "How'd they end up here?"

"Same way as I did. They were victims of plunder, crewmembers on some of the ships my father overtook. They fled the Nevervoid and sought asylum here before the ageless island could claim any more of their lives. Rhys was only eight." She motions to the young boy with the spyglass. "The *Wendy Bird* has given them a chance at life again." She sighs, meeting my gaze. "If I've learned one thing, Pete, it's that growing up isn't the problem. Thinking you can outrun it is."

I nod solemnly. "My father often said the same thing to me when I was just a child."

"Don't be afraid to grow up, Pete my boy, but stay curious. Always stay curious. The stories keep us young." It was true. I'd read enough to expand my imagination all my life and even into my mid-twenties. I'd never lacked curiosity or wonder despite the aging of my limbs, much to Beverly's chagrin. *"It's not so much the body we need to keep young, but the mind."*

My father was right yet again.

"I think you and my dad would have gotten along," I say to Estella. "He would have liked you."

She looks at me and smiles. "It sounds like I would have liked him, too."

The brazen thunder of Taurus bellowing behind us makes me jump, breaking the magic of our conversation. I turn to see the large bull scuffing his hoof against the inky grains of the sky, impatience brimming from his heated eyes.

"Took you long enough to acknowledge me, Star Boy. Wouldn't you like to know my name?" The bull shakes his head and swishes his tail as if he is swatting away flies.

"Yes, I suppose that's why I'm here." I step forward, taking in the sheer size of the bull before me. Upon closer look, his coat is a deep maple-brown, and his girth is about the size of Big Ben back home. "What's your true name?"

"Bannock Beasty." He bows his head, snuffling.

"Like the food?" I try to keep from laughing.

"My favorite kind. Though I prefer mine made with stardust. Can't abide that grainy stuff you humans call edible."

Then I do laugh, loud and clear. Estella joins in beside me.

"You humans are such odd creatures." Bannock snorts, twitching his head.

"Come, Pete." Estella takes my hand once more. "There's still more to see."

I nod, waving goodbye to Taurus—*Bannock*—and head back to the ship's wheel. Estella's hand is still in mine, and for some reason, she doesn't seem eager to let go.

"Where to next?" I ask.

"I was thinking Orion or Castor or…" She trails off, biting her lip.

"Or what?" I watch her closely. I have a feeling I know where this is headed.

"Well, I'm not ready now, but I… I think if you were with me, maybe I could face my father again…"

"You want me to go with you to the Nevervoid?" I'm as intrigued as I am shocked—and honestly, thrilled—at the prospect.

Though after what Estella's told me, perhaps I should be more afraid.

"Aye. If you are willing." She bites her lip again, awaiting my response.

I give her hand a reassuring squeeze, nodding. "You have my word."

And there, with the wheel grasped in one hand and Estella's in my other, I feel ready to chart this new course. Estella may be from the Nevervoid, but London blood goes deeper.

We'll set these stars ablaze, and maybe we'll even have a chance at setting her father free.

Part Three

~

The Nevervoid

With Estella's previous concern of running right into it, one would assume finding the Nevervoid to be easier than it is, but countless turns about the starlit night prove our journey difficult.

We've already made acquaintance with Orion, who is actually *Gallahad*, and Castor, who goes by *Matthias*. I had great satisfaction in learning their true ancestry and listening to their stories, but after spending countless nights in the skies and learning all the stars' names, Estella told me she was finally ready.

Thus, our journey to find the Nevervoid.

The closer we approach the elusive black hole, the harder it is to see where we are going. The harder it is to even navigate the *Wendy Bird* at all.

"Is this how you remember it?" I ask, my grip firm on the wheel as turbulence shakes our wooden craft.

Estella's right beside me, her eyes wide and her hands finding the nearest thing to hold onto—my arm—so she doesn't fall. "I can't recall. It's been years since I first entered it, and I've never been back, least of all with the *Wendy Bird*."

I figured as much. Still, if we're to make it through and have any hope of liberating her father, this wingless ship had better remain intact and not turn to stardust beneath our feet.

Suddenly, my stomach drops to my toes as the *Wendy Bird* nose dives into even deeper blackness.

Estella screams next to me, her hand gripping my bicep tighter, and I suck in a breath so as not to share in her fear. *We will not die. Not up here.*

"Is the anchor hoisted? Are the sails still taken in?" I call into the night, hoping the crew hears my plea for help. Anything to keep us from dipping further and moving at an unholy clip.

We will not die, I repeat to myself. *Not among the stars I've learned to call home.*

I try cutting the wheel, but it remains locked in place. It doesn't budge, despite my best efforts. I'd have greater luck uprooting a tree. "We're getting sucked in," I say, my heart hammering against my chest.

"Perhaps," Estella begins, "perhaps this is normal."

"Normal?" I raise my eyebrows.

"Yes, but only in part." She sucks in a breath and then expels it at once. "I just remembered something!"

Time seems to freeze between us, our rapid descent and the gut-churning feeling in my stomach the only things reminding me time is still going.

"What is it?" I feel ten years old again, asking my father to divulge his secrets—about the stars, all his stories. An urgency not born of impatience but of wonder. A desire to understand.

"Stories," she says, and for a second I think she's reading my thoughts—again. She squeezes my arm. "The stories, Pete! The stars tell their stories, and the Nevervoid is telling you hers. In order to enter it, we must listen, not fight it. Let go of the wheel."

I do as she says, hesitant at first, but then the turbulence abates. Suddenly, the once-black abyss is dotted with pricks of white. Then pink. Then cobalt blue. And then a whole host of colors starts whizzing past the *Wendy Bird*, reaching and shimmering with wispy arms like the aurora borealis against the backdrop of an ebony sky.

I watch in awe, too mesmerized to feel any fear.

Across the expanse of dancing colors reveals the likeness of a flying stork carrying a package in its beak. Another color whizzes by and shows that same stork caught in a lightning storm, dropping the package and seeking shelter. More pigments stream through the air, showing the package falling, opening, tumbling through the inky blackness of the celestial sphere. Another swatch of colors reveals its contents: seeds the consistency of stardust, and as they scatter, things begin to solidify and grow. But it's not just plants and flowers; there are rivers and lakes, a sun and moon and stars, rocks and mountains, birds and beasts, and finally an island sitting in the middle of a vast ocean.

Is this…what is this?

Estella gasps next to me. "It's the beginning."

The beginning?

"I've forgotten until now. This is how the Nevervoid came to be. That stork must have gathered some of Aquila's eggs."

I scratch my head. I'd heard of Aquila, the golden eagle, and had studied the constellation countless times, but about her eggs…

"I know what you're thinking." Estella faces me, searching my gaze as the *Wendy Bird* glides gently through the remaining host of colors. "But her eggs aren't like the ones down there." She points beyond the deck of the ship to London below, now just a tiny pinprick of light from our distance. "Her eggs are like seeds, and they grow into magical things, not strictly more fowl. That's how I claimed my magic."

I only nod, staring at the woman before me, her green eyes shimmering amidst the last rays of the aurora borealis. If I wasn't already made aware of her humanity, I would think she belonged here just as much as the stars did with the way she converses amongst them, telling their tales as if they were her own.

I feel drawn to her, much like a bee to a flower, the two having been made for one another since the beginning of time despite their obvious differences. We seem to understand one another. Like my mother and my father had.

I swallow at the realization, taking a timid step toward her when suddenly there's light.

Blinding, sun-filled light cascades through the blackness.

Squinting, I hold a hand up to shield my eyes, gently guiding Estella to stand behind me in case of what's to come. The effulgent brightness increases before it begins to diminish, and when it finally lifts, a whole new world comes into view.

"We're here," she says over my shoulder, her words laced with anticipation. Or apprehension.

I look at her, and she nods before grabbing my hand. We walk to the edge of the deck and peer over the side.

A vast ocean speckled with countless ships stretches below us, and at its center lies a mountainous island. The land is green, golden, and lush, and I can already tell it's well-watered with the amount of vegetation and birds darting through the skies. Animals need food, and this land looks bountiful enough to supply it in spades.

How about the people? I wonder if there are any others besides Estella's father living here.

The air feels both heavy and light at once, as if I can feel the effects of agelessness begin to creep into my bones, all the while time still moves forward at a steady rate. It's jarring, to say the least.

"So, what do we do now?" I ask, uncertain of how to get this pirate ship made of stardust down to land.

"Why, the ladder, of course," Estella says as if it's the most obvious solution. When she sees the confusion on my face, she continues, "It's a magical ladder, and it stretches depending on the distance required of it. We'll bring the *Wendy Bird* a little closer, and then we'll take the ladder the rest of the way."

I nod, marveling at this magic ship and feeling a bit disjointed from all the things I have yet to learn.

Estella squeezes my hand. "Sorry, Pete. You're such a natural that I forget you're new here. If it's any consolation, the *Wendy Bird* hasn't flown this well since I acquired her." She pauses, looking at me with something akin to admiration. "She likes you."

Her praise warms my chest, and I can't help wondering if she's really talking about the ship.

Estella's cheeks redden as if she's just thought the same thing, and she snatches her hand away. She addresses the rest of the crew and prepares them for our departure.

By the time I navigate the *Wendy Bird* to a decent landing spot, Rhys has the rope ladder cascading down its port side.

"Best of luck, Captain! Miss Estella!" Rhys says, smiling at us both with his spyglass tucked beneath his arm.

The two of us descend the ladder; I go first just in case she should fall. When it feels like an eternity has passed, my feet finally hit something solid. The smell of earth wafts beneath my nose, the scent of springtime and new growth. Estella is right beside me, her expression guarded. She's no longer the carefree girl she was on the *Wendy Bird*.

"Ready—?" I begin, stopping short at the sound of a snapping twig and a rustling of leaves.

Estella's sudden intake of breath doesn't bode well.

I turn and follow her gaze. Her hand is like iron in mine, squeezing hard. So different from her nervous grip or her reassuring one on the *Wendy Bird*. No, this one is fueled by fear *and* fire.

"Well, look who's returned," a deep voice says. "The wayward daughter of Jasper Hook."

Part Four

~

Jasper

A man, who looks to be in his late thirties, steps out from beneath the shadow of a tall golden maple and stands before us, his green eyes a direct match to Estella's. His hair is jet black and coarse, as if the sea reached out and stroked its watery fingers through it and curled each strand piece by piece.

"Father," Estella rasps. She clings to my side.

"Welcome back, my Stellarlune," Jasper says, his voice gentler than I would have imagined it to be.

Stellarlune. Star and moon. How apt the nickname is for Estella; though by the way she tenses beside me, I'm not so sure she's happy to hear it.

"How did you know we were coming here?" she asks.

At this, he finally notices me, giving me a once-over before answering her question. "I saw the Argo Navis enter the atmosphere. Hard to spot a glittering ship. But tell me, who have you brought with you?" His eyes still haven't left mine.

My chest feels tight.

"This is Pete." She loosens her grip, cheeks reddening, and takes half a step away.

I miss the warmth of her hand.

"Pete," he says. "Pete…?"

"Peter Parrel." I extend my hand.

He doesn't shake it. The surname seems to strike a chord, though, for Jasper raises a brow. "Interesting. I knew a Parrel once. Long time ago, I'm afraid."

"What was his name?" For some reason, I need to know. My father passed away when I was sixteen, and my mother only a few years after that, and yet I still feel both their losses keenly. The stars remind me of them, and I know my father would have given anything to be amongst them like I am now.

"Peter, much like yours," Jasper says.

My father. Jasper Hook knew my father.

"Good man, he was. Is. I assume your old man is, well, *older* now than he was back when I last saw him. If I recall, he liked the stars, too. You should have brought him with you to keep from the blighted aging." Jasper smiles wryly, a smugness to his exterior that doesn't sit right with me.

I suddenly understand why Estella is so uncomfortable in his presence. Jasper is so obsessed with his youth that he is hardly paying attention to his own daughter.

I clear my throat. "Was," I correct. "My father passed away

years ago. And though he'd like it here, I know he wouldn't want to stay." *Not like you.*

My father was wise; he wouldn't choose to laze away in some ageless void, even if it *was* set amongst the stars. He wasn't that sort of man. Besides, stories are ever changing. One needed to experience life in order to tell them.

"Ah, well, my condolences." Silence hovers between us at his extension of sympathy.

After a beat passes, Estella cuts in. "I've come to take you home, Father." Her voice is timid at first but then grows in confidence. "London misses us. I want to go back. With you."

Go back to London? For some reason the news smacks with reality. But of course! It's not like Estella will remain in the heavens forever, even if she does belong more to the stars than to the earth.

"Home?" Jasper scoffs. "I am home." The line of his jaw hardens and the gentleness of his words is replaced by something bitter. He doesn't meet her gaze.

"What does this place have to offer you but lost hopes and dreams? Life is empty without companionship. Without..." Her voice grows hoarse. "Without family." Estella looks close to tears, and I can tell her father's choices pain her more than her words convey. "You've kept me from mine for the past thirty years. All my cousins will be older than me by now. Friends won't remember who I am. You've taken so much from me, Father."

Again, weighty silence stretches on with her admission.

She clears her throat, pressing her luck. "But if you were to come back with me, we could ease into the changes together." Something akin to hope shines in her eyes. "We could resume life as normal—"

"No." His one word is like a saw.

"No?" And Estella is the felled tree.

He still won't meet her gaze. Either he's a coward or his heart is too calloused by his pride. "There is no normal."

She blinks, taken aback. "You're okay with this, then?" She looks as if she's been dealt a tremendous blow. He doesn't answer. "Father?" Estella's fists clench by her sides. "Look at me!" she cries.

Jasper lifts his head. What I expect to see is disdain, but instead, there's a brokenness and weariness in his eyes that boasts years of pain despite the longevity the Nevervoid is giving him.

Estella doesn't wait for him to answer as tears stream down her face. "You're okay with remaining as you are while your only child surpasses you in years? Dying before you even take your last breath?"

Jasper pales. "That's why I brought you here, Stellarlune. To live together and protect you from dying. Don't you see? The Nevervoid can grant us that! We'll never have to succumb to your poor mother's fate."

The pieces are slowly coming together. The more I observe Jasper, it's evident he hasn't healed from his wife's death. His rash decisions stem from a still-broken heart and a fear of dying. And he's grown greedy because of it.

"One can't outrun the inevitable, son. It's better just to live to the fullest and tackle the obstacles as they come." My father's words ring clear in my head even now. His wisdom seems to find a home no matter the scenario.

"I choose to *live*, Father. Really live. I won't have the Nevervoid take that from me again by granting me something unnatural. I'm not afraid of dying. I'm afraid of remaining as I am and growing cold because of it."

"I don't know any other way, Lune. I've made my choice, and I'm bound to keep it. A lost man in the Nevervoid." His voice trails off.

"But it doesn't have to stay this way." She takes a timid step toward him. "Aren't I enough for you?"

Now he looks wounded. Pained beyond measure. "You've always been enough for me, Estella. More than. Why else do you think I acted as I did?"

"Then why won't you come?" she pleads.

"This is my home now." He gestures to the island around him—to the towering trees, the crystal blue of the nearby ocean, the fleet bobbing in the surf—as if it is proof enough. "I belong *here*."

Estella brushes at her tears, inhaling slowly. The hope in her eyes withers.

"Even if I were to go with you, I'm not sure I'd know how," Jasper continues. "I want to be a part of two worlds, Lune. Yours and the Nevervoid. And I've come to terms with the fact that I can't have both."

I frown. Life is full of sacrifice; oftentimes we aren't meant to have it all. Would Jasper ever see that?

I clear my throat, unsure if I should speak but feeling as if I can't help it any longer. "The Nevervoid will always be here, Jasper. But your daughter won't. Do you want to live your years alone and lose the time you could have spent with her? I can only imagine that sort of life would be one filled with regret. And that's something the Nevervoid can never cure."

Jasper looks at me, hard. And for once, he doesn't retaliate.

Estella gives me an appreciative glance, pressing my hand with her own.

I spoke what needed to be said, but it isn't up to me to change someone's heart. I can only plant a seed.

In the lingering silence, Estella takes another step toward her father. "Life is too short to hold onto regret, Father. That's too big a burden to bear. And you've been carrying it for far too long on your own."

Jasper looks like he wants to say something, but then his shoulders slump forward, the fight suddenly leaving his body. "I miss her so much, Stellarlune," he rasps. Tears pool in his eyes, and Estella runs to him. When she gathers him in her arms, he silently sobs, the only indication that he's crying the shuddering movements of his back and shoulders. He's a broken man amidst a life he's built for himself—a cage of endless regret and reminders that things could have been different.

After a few moments, he pulls away, wiping a hand across his nose and looking much less intimidating. If anything, he appears lighter. When he looks at Estella, there's a vulnerability in his gaze that wasn't there before. "Will you ever forgive me, Stellarlune?"

"For what, Father?" she asks.

"For all the ways I've hurt you. I only wanted to protect you. I—" He shakes his head.

"I forgive you." Estella doesn't hesitate, wiping the tears from her eyes. "But does that mean… Will you come home?" she asks, a hesitation there.

Jasper looks at me, at the *Wendy Bird*, and then finally at his daughter. "I don't know." His head wags again, but his gaze isn't hard as it was before.

"Please?" Estella presses. "Father?"

Jasper shifts on his feet. "It's been too long. I've no job. No means of resuming a life I've left behind. I've forgotten what it's like to age."

Estella takes her father's hand in both of hers. He looks at her with pleading eyes. "I'll be right there with you," she assures him. "We can grow old together."

"But how will I make a living? I've no resume—"

"I'd like to help, if I may." I take a step forward and summon my courage before clearing my throat. "I'm a manager at the Royal Observatory Greenwich in London, and we're in need of another astronomer. Someone who knows the stars. What better man for the job than someone who's lived amongst them for years?"

Jasper studies me with an unreadable expression, and I wonder if his tongue is trying to catch up with his brain. "I don't need your pity—"

"You'd be helping us more than us helping you," I add.

He purses his lips in consideration. "Greenwich, you say?"

I nod. Estella looks between the two of us, watching our exchange carefully.

"I guess it could be a possibility." He sighs, taking a look around him, observing the land he's inhabited for the past thirty years. "I could always come back. To visit."

Estella squeals with delight. "Does this mean you'll come,

Father? To London?"

Jasper squeezes his daughter's hand. "Aye, Stellarlune. I'm willing to give it a try."

Hope rises in my chest, and the smile on Estella's face is worth all the trips to the stars. "Great!" I extend my hand, and this time, Jasper takes it. "Welcome to the Royal Observatory Greenwich, Mr. Hook! How soon can you start?"

Jasper cracks a genuine smile. "Depends. How fast does your *Wendy Bird* fly?"

The End

Captain Maverick of Tarkin

(A steampunk misadventure)

Pull right, pull right!" I yell the warning amidst whirring cannon fire. My teeth are clenched to the point that I can taste blood, and my gaze remains locked on the vessel trailing behind us.

They won't take our ship down. They can't.

Kip tugs hard on the rudder, shifting his weight to my side. The singular piece of wood moves accordingly; the ship dips slightly in the wind, turbulence rocking the flying craft as it changes direction.

Just in time.

An iron ball slices through the air, missing the canvas keeping our craft afloat. A few more feet and the propeller would have been lost. The cannonball continues onward and grazes the top of the ship in front of me, but it's not enough to create any lasting damage.

Another rips through the air.

"Left!" I call.

This time, Kip pushes the rudder away from him as the iron ball shoots past our craft. The sudden change in direction jostles the steamship, and I grip its edge, every muscle tight as adrenaline pulses through my veins.

When will this madness end?

"Captain, how much longer can we last? The fleet…we've never been pursued like this before!" Kip shakes beside me.

I know.

His hands are chapped from manning the rig amidst these blistering winds, and his eyes are ripe with concern. He's young—younger than most for a first mate. At fourteen, he has every right to be afraid.

A quick glance to my left reveals the other airships struggling to keep afloat, dodging the ensuing attack from behind. He's right. In all my years as captain, the fleet has never been pursued this aggressively.

I raise my spyglass hastily and assess our odds.

The enemy is gaining. We're as good as dead men.

I set my jaw, stuffing the instrument under my arm. I run toward the panel of controls at the front of the ship: levers, knobs, keyholes, and buttons beckon to be pushed and maneuvered. *So it's come to this. We have no other choice.* I clamp down on the nearest lever, and the nose of the vessel suddenly lowers.

"What's going on?" Kip calls behind me.

"We're disappearing."

"But, Captain…the Cloudstream—"

"I know what I'm doing, Kip."

The airship descends among the clouds, and the rest of the fleet follows my lead, copying my every move. I need to protect them. My people of Tarkin—the black wing. This fleet is all that we have left.

Cannon fire resounds behind, but the deafening blasts dissipate in the thickening fog. As the clouds condense, I can see and hear nothing.

All is quiet.

I tap the dial to my left, and lights pop up, showing the connection is still strong. I count eight blinking green dots. Eight dots for eight ships, and I, their leader, reside in the ninth. All is under my command. Everyone is safe. For now.

It wasn't supposed to be this way. When a level-eight airquake tore through our country, the land split beneath us, crumbling and giving way to gravity. Most fell to their end, including half of my block, Kip's parents, my wife… We only had so much time to board the ships. To get to safety.

And captain was a title I had little choice but to accept. I was nominated by a unanimous vote despite my reluctance. Once a deckhand, now Captain Maverick of Tarkin.

It's been two years since that day, and the memories still haunt me. Two years on these blasted vessels. Two years with no place to land. The Fleet of Tarkin has served as our home and a reminder of all that we've lost.

The black wing painted on our sails was never supposed to be more than mere symbolism, but now we've become birds ourselves. Peregrine falcons, forever taking to the skies. Determined to survive.

We've been dealt a living hell, and the relentless brigade behind us proves yet again how luckless we are. They are the Vulkra: air raiders.

Where they come from remains a mystery, but it's rumored they make their home in the glacial frosts of Pavrost, a land as cold as their hearts. They patrol the Drifthold Airway and the edge of the Cloudstream, preying on the unsuspecting. I've been aware of them for months, but we can avoid this passage no longer. Not when the promise of safety lies on the other side of it. I've heard word of a new land, another floating haven, somewhere past the last beams of the far-reaching sun. And it's there where we are headed.

If we don't die first. The Vulkra have pushed us into dangerous, mind-numbing territory.

"Steady, Kip. Turbulence is picking up." He grips the rudder while I insert a key into one of the keyholes and twist. In that same moment, horizontal poles veined with canvas unfold from the sides of the craft like a pair of wooden wings in an effort to stabilize our erratic movements. I'm still clutching the lever in an iron grasp, the long scar trailing up my hand and forearm popping white amidst the strain. I'd gotten it back when Tarkin fell…another reminder that I'd failed to save my wife.

The memory haunts me.

"Maverick, help!" she screamed.

"Hold on, Nell! Don't let go!" I leaped a chasm and ran to my wife, dangling like a ribbon on a kite's tail. I grabbed her hand and tried pulling her up when I was dealt a tremendous blow to my right side. A rock wall crumbled on top of me, and my arm was impaled

by stones, my vision swimming in a blur of colors.

My hold faltered. My cursed fingers struggled to maintain their grasp.

"Maverick!"

And then Nell fell. Her grip slipped out of mine, and she tumbled off the edge of the world.

Gone.

I swallow back the acrid bile climbing up my throat, tamping down the painful memory. The guilt. The shame. I massage the space above my eyes and address Kip beside me. "Check on the others."

He nods, making for the hatch in the center of the deck. He lifts the wooden door and descends, disappearing as quick as lightning. Not even ten minutes later, he's by my side again, his face pale.

Something's wrong. "Out with it, lad." I direct the airship through a thicker cloud, my hand twitching on the lever; I'm not quite ready to stop our dive to safer territory. But something's clearly amiss. I can barely see the green dots blinking on the dial before me. *Am I seeing this right? Only seven now?*

"Serena. She says we're not safe." Kip rubs the back of his neck.

I resist rolling my eyes. "Of course we're not safe!" I bark.

"But it's Serena… She sees things…differently, you know."

True. Having an old woman with *the sight* has its advantages. But most often she speaks the obvious. I'm convinced her 'sight' is one born of senility rather than a gift.

"Listen, Kip. We need to make it through these clouds in order to get to this new country." *New country. Solid ground. Home.* "And we can't stop because the Vulkra will shoot us down before we make it out alive. I know what I'm doing." I clutch the lever harder, my nerves twitching.

That's a lie. I don't know what I'm doing at all.

Ever since I became captain, I've been tasked with saving the people I'd failed to protect before. And they depend on me—*me*— to bring them to safety.

But I couldn't save them all. Couldn't save my Nell.

Another look at the dial reveals only six green dots now, their frantic lights blinking in the haze. Suddenly, they shift to five dots and then four…three…two…one. My stomach drops to my toes.

I've lost connection with the fleet. My control over their vessels is gone. With no captain, their ships float aimlessly through the Cloudstream…or worse. *No. I can't believe that.* They can't have fallen, submitting to gravity's pull.

And then my connection disbands altogether. The system blacks out, the lever snaps upward and remains locked in place, and the airship lurches forward before dropping to a snail's pace. My hand still grips the wood fibers of the mechanism, unwilling to accept what's just happened.

All that's left moving is the propeller above, churning slowly with emergency power. Its every rotation is the only thing keeping us airborne.

"What's going on?" Kip looks at me, his eyes wide with horror.

He's too young for this. Just a mere boy.

Fear grips my throat, and my past failings flit across my vision in one grisly strand. I swallow hard. "Looks like a change of plans, lad."

"A change, Captain?"

"Aye." I clutch the lever even harder, the white scar mocking me with its crude smile and sadistic truth. "We won't be going home after all, Kip. None of us will."

"But…but this can't be it," Kip says. "Can it?" His voice comes out in a tremor, and the sound of it breaks my heart.

"There's nothing else we can do. We're stranded, and the rest of the fleet is, too, if gravity hasn't already had its way with them." I run a hand over my face, sighing. *This is too much.*

Is it even worth lighting the emergency lamp? Would it be seen amidst this dreadful haze? I try yanking the lever once more, but it doesn't budge. I pound my fist on the control panel, and the lights don't even flicker.

Everything is over. *I've failed again.*

Oh, Nell.

Kip suddenly moves past me and stands at the nose of the ship. He squints his eyes and tilts his head to the side as if listening. "Do you hear that?" he asks.

"Hear what?" Have the fumes from the Cloudstream gone to his head? But his question sparks a reckless nerve inside my chest. More cannon fire? Have the Vulkra attempted to come after us even in *this*?

"Voices," he says. "It sounds…it sounds like singing." Kip cups a hand around his ear and leans into the wind.

"Careful, son. You're no use to the fleet if you fall." That's the last thing my conscience needs.

"Listen, Captain. You'll hear them, too."

"I don't have time for this rubbish, Kip. I—" My words stop

short, for in that moment, I do hear something. Something pleasant. Melodies on the wind, traveling through the thick clouds and nestling first inside my ears and then my chest.

Life.

Unless the Vulkra learned how to sing…

No. I recognize the song. It's Tarkin's national anthem, the hope of my people.

They're alive!

"It's the fleet." *Or one of them, at least.* The admission tastes of hope as I let out a shaky breath. So they haven't fallen. They haven't disappeared for good.

And they need rescuing!

Kip whoops loudly, throwing his hands in the air in relief. "We have to do something!" He maneuvers behind me, rifling through what little contents we have onboard. A mallet, a pair of goggles, and a saber all go flying on the deck behind him, his search proving futile.

"What in the airstream are you doing, lad?" I quirk a brow, watching him.

"Assessing our horde." Kip lifts a pack of seed cakes and tosses it aside.

"For what purpose?"

"How else do you think we'll be able to gather the fleet?" he asks.

I tip my head in a direction over his shoulder. "I was thinking with some rope." It's a ludicrous idea, but I'm not known for strategy. I see opportunities and wish for the best.

Hearing my fleet raise the cry of Tarkin, something stirs inside my chest. I *will* get my people to safety. With every last breath I have in me.

Kip's eyes dawn in understanding. "Brilliant, Captain! Why didn't I think of that?" Then his brow dips. "Er. Um. How exactly will the rope help?"

"First, let's light the lamp." I hope this works. *It has to work.* Upon seeing the captain's signal, the rest of the fleet should follow suit and light their lanterns in turn. A sign that they're alive, that they see the captain's signal and call for his aid.

I strike a match and fit the flame inside the glass. I rotate an external dial, and the fire catches on the gas, igniting the lantern into a full array of brilliant light.

"See anything yet?" I ask over my shoulder while I tend to the flame.

"Not yet, Capt—wait!" Kip leaves my side and stares into the clouds. "Over there!" He points in the direction of the nearest light.

I turn, thinking I'll have to squint, but the light isn't as small as I assumed it would be. In fact, it's a lot closer than I'd imagined.

With the voices still singing and the lantern now showing a clear path to our first ship, hope swells within me. This might be possible after all.

"Quick, hand me the mallet, Kip," I say, gathering the long coil of rope in my hands. What I'd give for a grappling hook or something sharper, but a mallet will have to do.

Kip hands me the item, and I attach it to the end of the rope, securing it with countless knots and prayers.

Then I call into the cloudy void. "Fleet of Tarkin. Can you hear me?" If I could make out any details of the ship, I'd call out the number painted on its side. But the light is the only thing visible.

The singing abates and turns into speech. "We hear you, Captain. Fleet number seven at your command."

Blessed be. "I'm tossing over a rope. Mind your heads." This is a tricky business. To toss the rope none too high as to puncture the canvas balloon above and none too low and risk losing our only means of rescue. "Hold the other end, will you, lad?" I address Kip, hoping our efforts don't prove disastrous.

I swing the rope back and send the mallet end flying. I keep waiting for it to go slack, but instead it feels like a weight pulling downward, taut as ever. To my horror, I realize I've missed.

"Keep your hold, Kip!" I scramble to clutch what I can of the rope myself.

We recover and try again.

"One more time." I send the rope flying, praying it hits the mark.

A resounding thunk echoes in the distance, and it's as beautiful as bells at Christmastide. Before I know it, we're being towed in toward ship number seven.

"Smart thinking, Captain. Losing the Vulkra and using the rope. How can we help?" a man named Grieg says.

"Is your crew secure below?" I gesture to the hold beneath his feet.

"As secure as they'll ever be. They were told to seek precautions. And to pray. For how else will we get out of this confounded mess?" He chuckles, cracking a smile in the midst of the foreboding Cloudstream.

"Right. Now to see about the others."

Grieg, his first mate Dori, Kip, and I set out to reclaim the rest of the fleet. It's tough work, but after all the lanterns are spotted, we work our way from one ship to the next, hoping and praying the rope is enough.

And surprisingly, it is.

In the end, the fleet is lined up in a row, nine in total, with Kip and I in the middle—four ships to our left and four ships to our right, all connected with ropes and anything we could find to bind our vessels together.

We float at a snail's pace, with our propellers spinning slowly above us, but at least we aren't alone. The crew cheers alongside one another, taking up Tarkin's anthem once again, and this time as one.

I swipe at a rogue tear. This devotion to our country, once fallen and exiled, lost but not destroyed, remains strong.

We haven't lost everything.

Not yet.

A throat clears behind me, and I realize it's Serena, her glossy, blind eyes somehow boring into my soul. She's as old as the day is long, her wrinkles housing decades of stories.

"Well done, Maverick." She's the only one who doesn't call me captain. It's both comforting…and unsettling. "You did it."

I open my mouth only to close it again, not quite certain what she means. "Did what?" I finally manage. If it's praise she's giving, I couldn't have done any of this without the help of the fleet. Especially without Kip's good ears. "It's really the crew—"

She waves her hand in the air. "Not *that*."

My brow dips. "But we're still in the Cloudstream. How is this worthy of merit?" *If anything, I got us stuck here. I'm actually to blame.*

"Oh tosh, none of that now." She swats my arm. "You've given us hope when we had none. You've saved us. And that, my boy, is something that can't be soon forgotten."

If only I could have saved Kip's parents. My sweet Nell.

"It's not your fault for those who were lost, Maverick," she says as if reading my thoughts. "And it still won't be should that happen now. But from the airquake until this very moment, you've led our people. You've given them a reason to hold on to courage time and time again. And that is a thing of hope, is it not?"

I don't know what to say. This praise feels too much, and yet her words make me feel lighter. As if my years of carrying shame and failure are seen for what they are and given grace.

"Besides." She cracks a toothy smile. "I have a good feeling about this."

"About what?" There's almost no point in asking because she'll tell me anyway. And most likely in a way that won't make sense.

"Come the dawn, just wait and see. The Cloudstream can't go on forever." Then she winks and walks away, aided by Kip, who helps her descend the ladder back to the hold.

She's senile, that's for certain, but her words spark something inside of me. They fill me with longing and dreams of a brighter future. And I can't help but wonder.

Though we may never reach the new haven, maybe there's still a point in trying.

It's too late to give up now.

Maybe to have hope is to have courage. To have wings.

Maybe that's enough.

The End

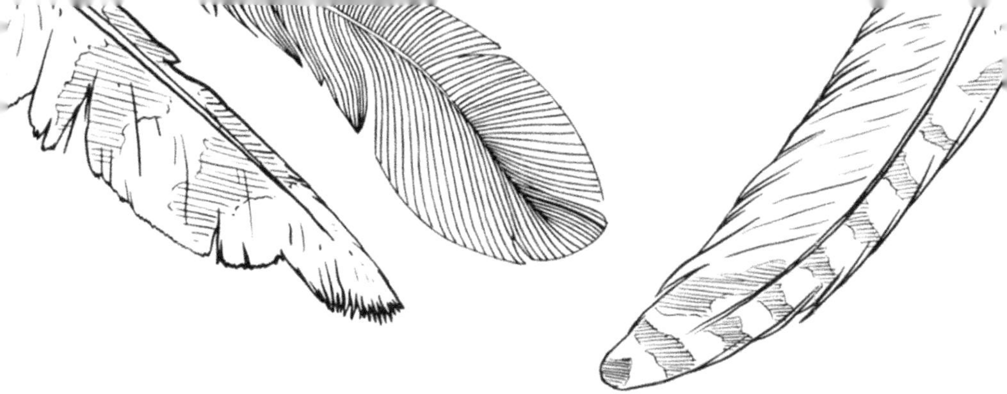

Romance

Second Chance Robin

(A second chance on love)

Y ou care for no one but yourself, Jett!" A bouquet of wildflowers gets shoved back in my arms. "One of these days, your self-conceit will come back to get you."

"Me?" *But I'm Jett Braxton. Nothing ever 'gets' me.*

"Yes, and I'll be ready to watch it when it does." My girlfriend of a whole two weeks, with tears running down her eyes, gets back inside her car and drives off, her tires screeching on the slush-filled road.

Good riddance, Astrid Blathe. With a name like that, I should have broken it off before it even started.

I kick at the ground and stare at her retreating car, puffing my cheeks out in the cold night air. After a few moments, I walk to the nearest street trashcan and dispose of the flowers before stuffing my hands in my coat pockets.

A sigh escapes my lips. Back to the drawing board, I guess?

Women fawn over me. I average a different girlfriend or two a month, and at this rate, I'll have had close to twenty by the new year. A record high since high school.

It's as if everyone wants a chance with Jett Braxton. *I don't mind it.* A stab of guilt niggles my conscience. *Mostly.*

I swat at a pretend fly even though it's the middle of winter, the action alleviating some of the tension in my chest.

The difficulty with women is that you can't read their minds. They can say one thing and it means something entirely different. How was I supposed to know Astrid loves flowers but is allergic to pollen, so much so that wildflowers make her eyes leak like a faucet? She should have told me she prefers fake ones.

Just like Kathy with her love of planes and fear of heights and Sharon with her need for warmth and fear of fire. They should've warned me…before I went skydiving with Kathy or started a bonfire in Sharon's backyard…

How am I supposed to get this whole dating thing right if all a girl wants is for me to *'pay attention'* as if I don't? I listen well enough. Well enough to know I'm too selfish to care for anyone but myself, that is. Or that I'm thoughtful in all the *wrong* ways. Astrid accused me of that very thing.

I run a hand through my hair. Maybe I'm not cut out for this sort of lifestyle anymore. No one seems to get me. Not since…

I shrug, shoving the thought aside.

Who needs a girlfriend anyway?

I don't need to make dinner reservations tonight, either.

I'll order out instead.

The walk back to my apartment isn't long, but with the soft snow flurries falling overhead, time seems to stretch. I round the corner of Pine and Ash and pause as if on instinct, the way I normally do every time I come this way. My apartment is only the next block over, but my eyes are drawn to the lights across the street, magical in their twinkling. It's the bookstore I pass at least twice a day to go to and from work: *Robin's Books and Gifts.* A place I've both admired and avoided for years.

Robin Guinevere Fay. *Now that's a name.*

Before I realize what's happening, I cross the street with my boots leaving subtle indentations in the slush behind me. It doesn't take long for me to stand outside the shop with my hand on the doorknob.

What on earth am I doing?

I suck in a breath and exhale deeply before walking inside. The shop bell jingles, alerting the store of my arrival. I force myself over the threshold before I have a chance to change my mind and high-tail it out of here.

Robin has been my best friend since we were kids. We grew up on the same street, laughed at the same jokes, ate from the same table…but something happened between us a few years back. Something I can't recall.

Why am I here again?

I'm single. I've moved on from Astrid…as of fifteen minutes ago. I'm not looking for a relationship, especially not in this place. Am I? The thought alone sends warmth to my cheeks, a feeling I'm not accustomed to.

Maybe this was a mistake.

I take a step back, ready to retreat but am stopped mid stride.

"Jett?"

Usually the sound of my name emboldens me, but this time, I feel paralyzed by who's spoken it. I suck in a breath and mentally slap my face, resolved to handle this like I would any other situation. I lift my gaze and meet hers—Robin Fay, the girl of my past. Her hair has lost the blonde I remember from high school and is now colored auburn like a robin's breast. *How apt.* It looks good on her. Too good.

I clear my suddenly dry throat. "Long time no see, huh?" I lean against a book display, giving off the award-winning grin I know the ladies love. Lips parted, the left half slightly higher than the right, brows dipped low… A few volumes of *The Secret Garden* tumble to the floor, and my facade cracks.

She crosses her arms and juts out her lower lip. "What are you doing here?" She sees right through me. She always has.

I straighten and pull at the collar around my neck. *Is it stuffy in here, or…?* I try clearing my throat again. "I was in the neighborhood—"

"You're always in the neighborhood, Jett." Her frown deepens.

She knows I live here?

As if seeing my confusion, she points outside. "I see you cross that street nearly every day. You live down Chestnut, apartment 20—what?" she snaps. "Why are you smiling like that?"

I can't help the smirk creeping up my face. *She watches me? As much as I watch her?*

"Can't keep your eyes off me, huh?" I waggle my eyebrows and catch the slow blush climbing her neck.

"No. That's *definitely* not it."

"Then still in the business of mischief, I see."

She shakes her head. "That was years ago. Just some childish antics. You, more than anyone, should know."

I *do* know. I was privy to many of her adventures and was often the instigator myself. We would get lost together in the woods, solving mysteries and trying to find secret passageways that led to hidden places. Much like in the book *The Secret Garden*, we'd always hoped to find a robin that would understand *us*, especially Robin herself, who already felt a kinship to the creature due to her name.

We spent so many summer days together; I pulled pranks and she retaliated. There was this constant ebb and flow, this understanding between us. Talking to Robin was never confusing. I knew what she liked, and she didn't expect more from me than what I could give. And it had always been enough…but then something changed.

Robin continues, breaking my stream of conscience. "Besides, I abandoned such foolish games to start my own business." She spreads her arms wide and then seems to think better of it. "I don't know why I bother telling you this, though."

"Why not? You used to tell me everything. We both did—"

"We were just children, Jett. We've grown up. Time changes things. *People* change." The way she says people sends a shiver down my spine, as if I'm the one she's talking about. And as if the change hasn't been a good one.

"Come on, Robbie." I try a different approach, instinctively reaching over and tugging on a lock of her hair.

She flinches, her fists clenched by her sides. "Don't—you know I've never liked that nickname."

There's that all-too-familiar temper I'm used to. I take it as a challenge; she always softens around me.

"What happened between us? Can't we be…you know, friends?" I give her my awe-inspiring smirk again, and it proves just as successful as the first.

"I'm not a kid anymore, Jett. You can play with all the girl's hearts you want, but you won't get to play with mine." She whirls in the opposite direction and begins fixing a shelf that already looks organized.

My smirk falls, and my hands go back to the collar at my throat. Her words suffocate me, and yet I still manage to speak. "I—I don't want to play with your heart, Robin."

She snaps her head up, and I see something like hurt in her eyes. "Then why are you here? To gloat over your many conquests and pretend like everything is all right?"

My face heats, and I can only imagine my resemblance to the common tomato has just increased by degrees. I've blushed twice now in the span of twenty minutes. Maybe I'm running a fever.

"No…that's not—I—" What can I say to this? I've dated many women, yes, but I can hardly remember all their names. Is that even a good thing? I just want to know what went wrong between us, why we've ended up like this. "What happened between us—"

"What happened? What happened is you got an inflated head and started schmoozing your way through high school. You dated every girl in our senior class. Every. Single. One. Then you went to college, and it only got worse. Did you ever consider… Did you even…?" She trails off, shaking her head.

Her words feel like I've been stabbed in the heart, and each time she speaks, it twists the blade deeper. "Did I what?"

"Did you ever consider the promise you made to me?" Robin moves away from the shelf and faces me fully now. "You said we'd be friends forever. That nothing could change that. But did you never once think of me as…as something more? How I might feel if…?" She stops short, biting her lip with eyes suddenly glossy.

I swallow hard. How had my actions affected her like this? I thought by leaving her alone, hers was the only heart I could protect. That hers was the one friendship I couldn't change, no matter how badly I wanted my hand at trying. Secretly, I'd always hoped for us to be something more.

I'm a fool.

"Every day." The words come out as a whisper. And as sincere as they are, they still feel rehearsed, like I've used them before.

Robin shakes her head. "I can't take you seriously, Jett. Your actions have always said otherwise. You can say all you want, but until you start *doing* something, I'll never be able to believe you." She walks closer and leans in a fraction as she peers up at me. There's a fiery light in her eyes, dancing despite her sorrow.

My heart speeds up, and I suddenly need oxygen.

"You know… I'd always wondered if there was something wrong with me…if that was the reason why you never dated me like the other girls." She pauses and drops her voice even lower. "But I was wrong. We may have played games as children, getting lost in our make-believe worlds in search of talking birds, but the biggest game you've ever played is promising something you could never keep."

She walks away, and my insides churn like a blazing volcano. This suddenly feels like life or death. Despite the anvil pressed against my heart, I need to say something. "Can you let me try again?" The urgency in my chest is like something I've never experienced before. I want to reach out to her. To hold her. To apologize for every stupid thing I've ever done to cause her pain. Heck, I'd even get her a pet robin if it made any of this better.

She stops moving but doesn't turn to face me.

With a fortifying breath, I approach her back but make sure to keep my distance. Something tells me the truth is the only thing that can help mend what's broken now. "Yours is the only heart I've ever wanted all these years, Robin." It's an admission I never thought I'd speak, let alone today of all days, but it's freeing. I swallow my pride and continue. "I was just too afraid to tell you. I didn't think I had a chance, so I dated other women."

"A lot of other women," she chimes in.

"Yeah." I rub a hand along the nape of my neck. "But that's beside the point. I dated a lot because I was a coward. And I bungled every relationship with my lack of interest, mostly because I think my heart had already chosen you." My words feel thick inside my throat. "I'm just sorry I hurt you instead."

Robin turns her still-glossy eyes on me. "How do I know I can trust you, Jett Braxton?"

"You can't." I pause, taking a deep breath and a step closer. "But I've spent too many years pretending to be something I'm not, and I'd like to try my hand at something new. Maybe I'll even become quite good at it." A smile escapes my lips, and I can tell it's of the genuine sort, all traces of my smirk gone. "Do you think you can give me a second chance, Robin? Can you forgive me?"

She looks wary; years of hurt won't disappear in a moment of honest contrition. I just hope she can sense my sincerity. She lifts a finger to her lips as if trying to cover a burgeoning smile, tapping it a few times, considering.

The silence between us feels like a chasm that could swallow me whole. But it's not entirely hopeless, for I feel something building between us once more. Like a robin and its nest.

"I think I'd like some help shelving some books out back," she says, "and then I'll let you know." She turns and walks away, but her steps are light. And I'm pretty sure I catch one of her genuine smiles in return.

Suddenly, it's like we're kids again. Traversing through a wood, searching for secrets and magicked birds in our make-believe worlds.

But this time, though I've got a lot to prove, it's no longer pretend.

If Robin's willing to give me a second chance, I won't waste it.

The End

The Swan and the Masquerade

(A Regency romance)

Present

I t's only the first dance, but I can already tell I'll dread the rest of the evening. Situated between the main stairwell and the thick crimson curtains that conceal a large bay window, I sit in a chair draped in velvet, staring out into a mass of people, all decorated in their fineries.

Men and women hide behind strange masks and exchange flirtatious glances and bows, thoroughly enjoying themselves as they willingly embrace, dancing in formation to the sound of stringed instruments and flutes. The pianoforte exudes cascading bass notes while the violins and woodwinds bounce around in a sporadic fashion, fighting for the melody while creating an atmosphere of euphoric exuberance.

The dancers partake in the music's jaunty tune, bending and twisting to the point of breaking, yet their motions are so fluid and light that I might mistake them for fairies. The women's gowns—gold, turquoise, sea-foam green, peach, magenta, and any other color imaginable—form a cacophonous medley to which my eyes have a hard time adjusting. The men sport white cotton shirts, cravats, and tan trousers all underneath black or navy waistcoats, failing to dull the dancing rainbow. It is all too much. The ladies twirl with an endless rhythm, giggling in hysterics to get their partners' attention while I just sit here, counting how many dances I must decline from overly flirtatious men.

Past

"Mother, why do you insist upon inviting these strange men over to our home? For the past two years they've done nothing but stare me down as I eat!" And because of this, I had lost enough weight to classify myself as a beanpole. I could feel the pin-straight, blonde hair atop my head start to frizz from anger and anxiety as my sweaty hands began to smudge the ink on the letter lying on my desk, one I hoped I would finally get a response to.

"Marianne, my dear, you know I want what's best for you, and since your father's passing, I fear the urgency in securing your future. Since you have made it clear that you would rather forgo the dances, I took matters into my own hands." She clapped a

decorative feathered fan in her freshly manicured fingers, running her nails through the plumage. *"I thought we had been over this already."*

It was true; we had discussed this on several occasions and agreed to disagree. At least it was better to have random men at our house for a quick evening meal than be subjected to an extravagant evening of humiliation elsewhere. At least I could hide in my room. It's not that I minded balls, but to my mother, they only served one purpose: marriage. Fortunately, I could keep greater distance from men at my house than I could at any ball by feigning a headache, allowing me more time to write letters or run through the hillside should I see fit. Still, I loathed her for it.

"But why? There is hardly a need. I don't want to meet men at the balls or at our home. I can make a living for myself by writing— you'll see. I won't change my mind, Mother. Please just let it go!"

My vision blurred, unnecessary tears forming in the corners of my eyes as they rolled off and furthered the smudge marks on my letter. She would never understand.

Present

My eyes sting even now. I touch the swan charm dangling from the bracelet on my wrist in hopes of shooing away bad memories and recollecting good ones. Sitting here for the past half hour has already heightened my nerves. The occasional glances of masked men and women that are thrown my way don't help either; they must be wondering why I've consigned myself to being a wallflower. The only reason my mask hasn't ended up in the nearest disposable is so I blend in; there's nothing worse than drawing even *more* attention at large gatherings such as these. But so far, I feel like a caged bird on display.

Ignoring their glances, I focus my attention on a waiter shuffling over with a half-empty tray of pastries. Three young ladies standing off to the side of me gape at the desserts and descend upon them like hungry hawks, stuffing mouthfuls of sweets into their gaping maws.

The waiter dishes out his last crème puff and stuffs the metal dish under his arm before he walks toward me, aware that I have been staring in his direction for the past five minutes.

"Sorry, miss, but it appears we are all out of pastries." The fact that he does not address me by my proper name means my disguise is working. "There shall be another tray coming out shortly." He bows, removing the metal dish from under his arm and placing it over his chest in a grand gesture. A pair of green eyes peering between a flux of peacock feathers and opal stones stares back at me, and it takes me a few seconds to realize it's my own reflection.

I look ridiculous.

Past

"But this is a fabulous opportunity for you, dear!" my mother said. *"Don't you see? At this rate, you'll have an offer of marriage before the strike of winter, and let's not forget your younger sisters. It would be a shame to see Harriet and Isabella married off before you. Isabella already seems to have made an impact on our young Greggory Hastings."*

"If they wait for me to marry first, they'll be waiting a long time, Mother. Besides, it would be better if you directed your dreams toward Harriet; she has more patience for such matters. I prefer my independence. Why can't you understand that?"

No matter how hard I pleaded, she wouldn't listen.

Present

The server leaves with his tray, and in his absence, I begin to focus my attention back on the dance. Scanning the room, I find my sisters enjoying themselves amidst the chaos. Both of their partners stand tall and broad, one wearing the mask of a bear and the other a fox. Harriet resembles a flamingo in her pink gown and matching mask, while Isabella sports a royal blue gown and mask that reminds me of the Hasting Estate's family bird, the Blue MaCawling. It has been Isabella's goal to ensnare Greggory Hastings since childhood, and her outfit choice makes her resolve all the more obvious.

The men are of noble birth, carrying an air of arrogance, but then again, my sisters aren't ones to care much for how their suitors act, especially not the dashing Greggory Hastings. Looks and status are everything to them, whereas I prefer a man with tact and a civilized mind that extends beyond physical appearance and money.

Though I've met a few who fit that description, I've only ever known of one man who meets those qualifications completely.

Harriet notices me and waltzes with the bear over to where I'm sitting; she stops long enough to bend down and whisper something into my ear.

"You'll never guess what I've just learned! There are rumors that Mr. Northington is to come to this very ball—tonight! I heard so from Miss Hastings herself. You know how she loves to gossip! She says he returned from Bath not two hours ago and should be on his way this very moment. The gumption of that man to join high society when he has no title and lives on thirty thousand pounds a year!" Harriet barks a laugh and then frowns when I don't reply. "Now don't look so dreadful, Mari. I thought out of everyone you would be happy to hear of your friend's long-awaited return, no matter how ill-fitting to society he is. My advice is to let him see you flirting and thriving so he'll know just how out of reach you are! And do smile; you look positively morose. Oh—Rupert, let's dance another!"

Forgetting she is speaking to me, Harriet quickly regroups with today's suitor—who I know now is Rupert—and joins the group already on the floor to dance the quadrille, all smiles and eagerness.

But I hardly care.

William? Here tonight? My heart races as I scan the room.

Past

"Because I want to see you well-off and taken care of. You don't have much time left, darling, whereas Harriet is two years your junior. Just think, our guest Mr. Blake gets seventy-five thousand pounds a year; doesn't that sound divine? His fortune could secure you for the rest of your life, not to mention our family! I don't want you wasting away like the Northingtons with their eldest son becoming an ornithologist. What a disgrace—such a trivial

occupation for a man—and don't even get me started about Christine. The scandal!"

"Mother, please! Don't speak of William or his sister that way. Christine is as admirable as they come; whatever happened was an accident. William is commendable in every sense, and any woman would consider herself most fortunate to find herself the object of his affection...or his friend..." When my mother's eyes narrowed at my blushing cheeks, I quickly continued. *"Besides, I don't care about how much money Mr. Blake has, but I do care that he's a loathsome pig. I just want these men to leave me alone because it's simply a waste of their time."*

I turned around in frustration. Despite my efforts in arguing with her, I knew deep down that she would never try to understand my heart.

I was immobilized in her calloused grasp.

Present

I've been sitting for far too long, so I decide to get up and attempt to leave the room. It has grown too humid in the matter of a few minutes, and running in the fresh air would be a divine escape. If I stay along the perimeter of the room, perhaps I will remain unnoticed. The veranda is only a breath away.

The sleek marble floors feel smooth to the touch on my bare feet, and the sparkling chandelier commands attention amidst the smaller wall sconces and candelabras on tables. Upholstered chairs rest in every corner of the room, and my goal is to leave mine and head for the comforts of the outdoors and run the length of the

Hasting's Estate.

Wild and free. With hopes of running away from William…or into him.

Clasping the swan charm on my left wrist, I feel my pulse beating wildly. I need to leave this room, for it has suddenly grown even warmer.

As I walk toward the door, I find myself searching, hoping, and anxious to see if my friend has returned.

Past

"Marianne," my mother spoke to my back, *"we agreed that I would grant you three years of avoiding the dances and parties, but in turn, you would allow me to invite these men over to the house until you accepted one of them as your husband."*

I had hardly agreed to that—I'd had no other choice.

"But I haven't accepted anyone, and our 'agreement' is more than halfway over. Besides, I'd rather eat a pig's slop than marry someone who calls himself a respectable man when he knows no meaning of the word. No matter what you say, it won't have the power to change my mind."

Ever since William left rather spontaneously for university, nothing had felt the same—our communication dwindled despite my attempts at the letters. But his attendance or absence mattered little to my mother, who only concerned herself with the affairs of a suitor's wealth.

I had put up with these men—some better than others— knowing it would amount to nothing, if only to appease her. And my heart had to suffer the consequences.

Present

The musicians take up another tune, sending the dance floor into a wild frenzy of jubilant clatter. Feet pound on the marble tiles, and their sounds echo throughout the entire hall, filling the dance hall with more noise. I'm halfway to the other side of the room when I spot my mother flirting with some older gentlemen near the white-bricked fireplace; I'm sure its warmth isn't the only thing making the men blush. I feel sorry for them.

If my father could see her now, her playful interactions would send him rolling in his grave—God rest his soul.

Past

"How revolting! Pig's slop!" I could imagine her hand flying toward her mouth in shock. *"You don't mean that, darling. Come now, show some civility and turn around to face me like the well-meaning daughter I know you can be."*

A long string of quiet lingered between us as I continued staring outside, the tension palpable. She hated to be ignored.

"Fine—insolent girl! I've had quite enough of your silence. I have been gracious to you, but my patience has grown thin, and you leave me no choice. It's back to the dances you go! I was going to wait until your nineteenth birthday, to give you one more year, but you have pushed my limits. In a fortnight, there is to be a masquerade ball at the Hastings' family estate, and I believe you'll

make a suitable bride at eighteen just the same as nineteen. For if you don't secure a proposal by the stroke of midnight on that very night, I have every right to choose your suitor and marry you off the following morning!"

I could feel her smug smile piercing through my back without needing to turn around; my chances of freedom were slowly diminishing.

"I should have made this decision a long time ago. Pity we've had to wait this long." She sighed. *"Do I make myself clear?"*

The devil himself wasn't made of stone this tough.

"You're impossible, Mother." Everything inside of me wanted to scream and rip my hair out, but I knew that furthering the argument would result in nothing.

So I continued to stare out the window.

Present

As I'm about to press open the door leading to my freedom on the veranda, something catches me by the hand and spins me in the opposite direction. My heart flutters but then nearly stops beating as I stare into the face of a pig-masked man. I wrench my hand from his grasp as quickly as it is taken up. His mouth gives him away.

"Miss Pembroke, I have been searching *ardently* for you all night! It seems many other men have already kept you occupied, robbing me of my chance to dance with such a fine beauty as yourself." His eyes rove over my figure in an unbecoming way; I'd rather have ants crawling on my skin. "My heart has been pining to see those lovely green eyes once more. Will you accompany me to this next dance?"

No, you absolutely may not. The thought alone makes my gut roil.

Past

"Ah, but what would you do without me? Come now, Marianne, get some rest. You have a big day to prepare for! In two weeks, Mr. Blake will be at the ball, and I want you to accompany him for as many dances as he asks for. If you refuse him, you'll receive further consequences we can discuss later." Mother's tone indicated that she was rather looking forward to what those consequences entailed.

She continued, *"He has his eyes set on you, my dear. Take advantage of it! For if you reject him, you may as well find yourself marrying him the next day."*

The sound of my mother's shrill laughter sent a shiver down my spine. Would this torture never end?

Present

My mouth hangs open, aghast at his forwardness. Mr. Blake exudes pompous flattery of the acutest kind. My skin prickles with disgust as I stare at his large, salivating mouth, where clusters of pimples dot his skin. I'd rather kiss a *real* pig.

I'm about to answer with a curt "perhaps another time," only slightly heeding my mother's warning, when something catches his attention.

"Mr. Blake! Oh, what a pleasant surprise!" A shapely brunette with exceeding bosoms and a perfect nose saunters over to him. Her large eyes and full lips make her look younger than she actually is. "Someone was just telling me about your summer home in Brighton—overlooking the ocean, I hear—what a marvelous sight that must be. And how the estate is worth more than all the men in this room combined. I bet it's heavenly!" She touches his arm, her motives clear. But I don't even care. Mr. Blake shifts his focus from me and engages in full conversation with her, smiling back with his lecherous smile. *Blessed be.* All I can think of is my freedom.

I breathe a sigh of relief.

Taking advantage of their obliviousness, I slowly back away and head for the veranda once more. This time, no one stops me.

I step out onto the cold stones, a reprieve from the crush. I make it to the banister, breathing deeply. There's something about the solitude of nighttime in contrast to the chaos of the indoors; sometimes I just need to leave it all behind.

Enjoying the stillness is long overdue, but it's just as quickly interrupted when something comes from behind, reaching for my hand. Again? I'm growing tired of this game.

"Will you never let me be?" I whirl around, about ready to club Mr. Blake in the face, when I am stopped short.

A tall man dressed in white coattails with matching trousers and shoes stands in my view. He is wearing a swan disguise, but that hardly covers his likeness, for I would recognize him anywhere. His honeysuckle curls cascade from behind the white feathers of his mask, and his ocean-blue eyes peep through the holes. His chin is strong, and his scruff only adds to his handsome face, making him look mature rather than older. The moonlight has a way of accentuating his every feature.

And once again, I am lost for words.

"I believe these are yours, miss." The gentleman gives a slight bow as he hands me a pair of evergreen slippers, the ones I had left behind under my now-unoccupied chair. I'd slipped them off and completely forgotten about them. "I'd recognize them anywhere." He winks, and my cheeks instantly warm.

It's true, I wore these shoes almost every day since I first got them five years ago, and he never let me live it down. Apparently, that would still be the case.

"But you always loved going barefoot more." A corner of his mouth tugs up in a smile, and my ridiculous heart beats wildly in response.

"Will!" I drop the shoes and embrace him, smelling the sweet scent of cinnamon and cedar on his skin. Just like I remember it—how I've always remembered it. "How good it is to see a familiar face!"

We each take a step back, giving each other some distance, though his hands seemed just as reluctant to leave my waist as mine did his. We're still standing close, though, enough that our breath mingles in the cool air. The blessed chill feels like a piece of heaven as the noise of the ball fades into the background. Under the sheen of twilight, it's just the two of us. The way it's always been.

"You look lovely tonight." He bends closer and whispers near my ear. "And I couldn't let Mr. Pigface harass you any longer for it. You seemed exceedingly uncomfortable with his attention." He leans back and lets out a string of fake snorts, his slightly crooked smile even more endearing now that I'd missed it for so long.

I laugh in response. "*You* sent that girl to distract him? I should have known!" I mockingly spar him in the ribs, looking up into his masked face. For a moment, I am filled with inexplicable joy; this is my Will, the one I had missed these past two years. But the longer I look, fear grips my core instead. *He's not mine. And he'll just leave again.*

I avert my gaze, pinpricks of tears dotting my vision. I should be happy to see him after so long. Instead, I'm crying. *Crying!*

"Mar? What's wrong?" William bridges the small gap between us, gently placing his hand beneath my chin and lifting my head. There's concern in his brow, and I so badly want to smooth the wrinkle out.

No. I should be upset. I am *upset.*

I allow the memories to creep into my chest. Hurt. Anger. Confusion. All I can think about are letters…all unreturned and ignored. Endless days of silence. Nothingness. I suck in a breath and let out the words that had been held hostage for too long. "You left—in the midst of things—you just disappeared. You left me." Admitting the words feels like reopening the wound. *Cripes these confounded emotions!*

"I didn't leave with the intention of hurting you, Mar. My parents were given a considerable donation, enough to send me away for my schooling. I don't know who my benefactor is, but apparently it was given under the condition that I take the money and leave the next day or I didn't leave at all. I took it as a chance to figure out my life. I had a lot of growing up to do." His gaze pierces my soul, a look that insinuates he too is filled with hurt. He wipes a tear from my cheek, and I try to move away but find that I can't.

I should be stronger than this, but his gentleness is my undoing. "You never wrote back. I thought you had forgotten about me." I desperately try building a cage around my heart as I stare into his eyes. Those beautiful eyes.

"Yes, I did! I responded to every single one. I never received a reply from you, and that worried me. I waited month after month and decided I couldn't bear it any longer. I was supposed to stay away for four full years; I've run the risk of ending my schooling for good now that I've returned prematurely. But I don't think I'll be going back any time soon. I made the trip home to Eastshire in hopes of figuring out the mystery of this blasted conundrum. And in hopes of seeing you again." He takes hold of both my hands and pauses when he sees my wrist.

A flutter of hope forms in my stomach. "So you didn't forget? How is it that our letters were never received? And why would your benefactor want to be rid of you from Eastshire like one would the Black Plague?" Something niggles the back of my mind. There's only one person in the world who cares so much about the whereabouts of William Northington, and it's to make sure he's as far away from me as possible.

"You're still wearing the bracelet I gave you." William gently lifts my arm to his eye level, playing with the charm.

"I haven't taken it off." It feels as though it's now become a part of me, an extension of my heart worn tangibly on my wrist. Despite being hurt by his leaving, I couldn't find it in me to ever take it off. What was surely just meant as a mere parting gift was something rendered much more significant upon its offering.

I remember back to when William had first given it to me.

We were walking the ruins of Grimfold Castle, rooks nesting in the crumbling towers and vines snaking up through the loose stones. It was a devastating type of beauty, the kind that left you bereft and in awe. We had chased each other through the walls of decaying rock, laughing heartily with the birds while listening to the waves crash against the crags.

If one stood high enough on the tallest part of the crumbling tower, one could see the flat moors stretching downhill and leading into the crystalline blue of the raging sea.

"Tomorrow," William said, *"we will explore the coast and find enough shells to make you a dozen bracelets."* He was thoughtful like that, but unlike most men I'd encountered, he actually meant what he said.

He held my hand as I descended the crumbling tower and settled myself on a fallen log. William sat next to me, the high grass brushing against our ankles. If my mother knew where I was, she'd surely give into fits. She was never keen on my friendship with William, but seeing as we were neighbors, there was little hope in stopping it.

As we sat there, I stared out toward the horizon and watched a brilliant magpie dancing in the air. I marveled at its freedom and grace as I scanned the tall trees before me, smelling the salt on the wind and feeling the warm sunshine beaming on my skin. Pretty soon I'd get freckles, another thing my mother loathed.

"Mar." This wasn't anything new. He'd given me this

nickname since we were children, and he'd been the only one to ever call me that since. But something in his tone indicated a sense of urgency. He reached into his pocket, and my heart began to pound.

What was he retrieving? I was not yet sixteen—still too young for marriage. But if he were to propose, how could I say no? I mean…we were best friends—

"I wanted to give you something." His words disrupted my racing thoughts, and I breathed a sigh of relief. A gift. That was something I knew how to accept.

He held out his hand, and a neatly wrapped packet fell into mine. I glanced at him, quirking my brow in question.

"Open it." He smiled.

I worked the string loose and peeled back the paper, revealing the object inside: it was a bracelet—a simple, yet beautiful bracelet with a little charm. Instantly, I knew he had made it. The thought sent a flurry of warmth to my middle, leaving me speechless.

"May I see your wrist?"

I placed my hand in his, the contact spreading warmth down my arm and into my middle. Why was I reacting this way? It was just William.

As he carefully worked the clasp closed on the delicate bracelet, I didn't miss the way his fingertips lingered briefly on my skin before he moved them away. The jewelry reflected the sunlight, the silver proven to have already bent to the will of its master.

"The charm is a swan, one of my favorite birds." He shifted his position and drew nearer.

William was deft with his hands and his eyes, which made

metalsmithing and bird-watching his primary hobbies; he excelled at both. And to have been given something that intertwined his two loves made me exceedingly happy.

"Will, this is beautiful, but why give it to me?" I couldn't help but wonder as I saw him growing restless. It seemed there was so much more he wanted to say but couldn't. Or wouldn't.

"A beautiful girl deserves something beautiful." He glanced up at me, and I caught my breath, his eyes betraying something deeper. He thought I was beautiful?

He reached toward my face and brushed a stray lock of hair behind my ear. His touch warmed my skin, and I found I couldn't look away, no matter how red my cheeks felt. Was he going to kiss me? I leaned in ever so slightly.

Before I had a chance to find out, he seemed to realize what he was doing and moved back, pushing to a stand. I didn't miss the subtle groan that left his mouth as he ran his hands through his hair. *"We should...head back."* It looked like he wanted to say something else, like something was warring in his heart. *"It's growing late."*

Not too late. More than anything, I wanted to stay outside and talk with him, to explore these new developments. Here, I felt free like the magpie, like the woman I was always made to be; inside held my mother and endless lectures on how to be a lady. And therefore, I was the captive.

But I had little choice.

William looked too distraught to be pressed any further; if there was something wrong, I trusted him enough to tell me.

"All right," I finally said.

On the walk back, I kept playing with the bracelet, telling myself that no matter what happened, it was staying on my wrist for the rest of my life.

And I'd somehow find out what was troubling William tomorrow.

Except that when the moon had gone abed, William had gone with it. And I'd never found the reason for his behavior.

"The swan. Do you know what it means?" William looks at me now, drawing my attention back to the present. He waits for my reply and continues once I shake my head. "It's symbolic. A promise of devotion. Of the heart.'"

A small smile escapes my once tear-streaked face. "I'm not sure I understand. Have I been carrying around someone's promise for these past two years?" Did I dare hope?

William's grin spreads wider. "Not just any promise, Mar. Mine—you've been carrying the promise of my heart since we were children. This bracelet is just a reminder of that. And I'd still like you to carry it."

He looks at me again, longing in his eyes. "I wish I was clearer with my intentions before I left, but I was immature and too foolish to realize that nothing should have come between our friendship. I was afraid and needed time to spread my wings, but my studies in ornithology helped me with that."

He winks again and smiles at his clever pun. "But truly, I am a blasted dolt. I've hurt you, and for that I'll never forgive myself. I spent hours apologizing in my letters, but I feared your heart had grown cold or you were simply ignoring me. Can you ever find it in your heart to forgive me now?" A sense of pleading escapes his eyes.

"I think I might be able to." I give him a teasing smile. "But first, why don't you ask me to dance so I don't have to be with Mr. Blake once he realizes where I've gone." I start laughing at the thought of having to dance with Mr. Pigface, trying not to stare at his ghastly chops. My mother will just have to deal with my disobedience.

But then another thought hits me. If I'm not proposed to by the stroke of twelve, I very well might be married to Mr. Pigface tomorrow. I often ignore my mother's disastrous plans, but something tells me I have little control over my fate. I'll be Mrs. Pigface before the sun has another chance to set.

"I can do that." William clears his throat and takes a step back—for all his humor, he looks unaccountably nervous. "Miss Marianne Pembroke, the fiery-willed girl from Eastshire, the woman who keeps me on my toes, the one who…"

"Will, it's just a dance. You can ask me plainly." I giggle.

"It's never just a dance with you, Mar." A corner of his mouth quirks up in a grin.

I never get tired of his smile.

But then he gets more serious, looking at me as if I'm the very air he breathes and he can't get enough of it. "Mar, do you know why swans are my favorite birds? Why they've been my favorite for years?"

For some reason my throat feels too tight to speak, so I just shake my head.

"It's because they are loyal to one another. When swans fall in love, they stick together for life; not even death can keep their love from dying. Nor distance from university." William pauses here, and my every nerve is tingling, my heart ready to burst at what he might say next. He swallows and continues. "That's how I feel for you, Mar. I have loved you all my life, from the moment I saw your hair get caught in that apple tree to when you sparred me in the ribs after grabbing your book. You're cunning, sweet, spirited, and you can spot the difference between a crow and a raven—which is no easy feat, mind you." He winks. "It would make me the happiest man if you would marry me and dance with me for the rest of my life." He gets down on one knee under the sheen of starlight, his eyes sparkling in the heavens' glory.

I don't even have a chance to process the joy before me when the door to the veranda bursts open and a slew of young ladies flounce outside. They pause at seeing William down on his knee, their hands toward their mouths, aghast, awaiting my response.

The music slows, and more people are staring the longer the door remains open. It seems the world has stopped, if only for a moment, for just William and me.

I feel as if I'm floating. Is it possible to be this happy? This isn't just any man asking me to dance—this is William Northington, *my* William. My childhood friend, the only man I've ever loved, who just asked for my hand in marriage.

A piercing scream breaks through the magic.

"No! Of all things holy and good—Marianne Juliette Pembroke!" My mother breaks through the group of girls and stops just inches away from us. "Don't you dare accept him! Think about what you're doing! I forbid you to say yes!" She wiggles her finger before my eyes before staring daggers at William.

I look from my mother back to my beloved, and a small smile spreads across my face. I'm too happy to cry, for the freedom I craved I have now been given full access to. I am the magpie. And with William, I'm also the swan.

I grasp his hand and squeeze it. "I have loved you for longer than I can remember, and I would happily be your wife." The words roll off my tongue, as wholesome and sweet as home-spun sugar. Words I never thought I would be able to say.

My mother shrieks in protest and stomps away while William closes the gap between the two of us. He scoops me into his arms, spinning me around as he plants gentle kisses on my hairline, cheeks, and nose. And finally, when we are left alone and all spectators have retreated indoors, William's mouth finds mine, and it's even sweeter than I imagined.

When we pull apart, our grins are as wide as the vast sky.

"I love you, Mar."

"I love you, too." It's always been him.

And just as soon as I've gathered my footing, I am spinning and twirling about the veranda once more, but this time I'm dancing, realizing this is the first man I haven't rejected within the last two years. The only man I have never rejected, not even once.

And I think that perhaps attending more balls in the future sounds like the most glorious thing in the world, especially if William—my swan—is by my side.

We'll be together until the end.

The End

Parched Sands

(A survival story)

My throat is parched like the ground beneath my feet. If I keep walking, maybe there's hope. It's the ones who stop moving who wind up kissing death.

Eighteen men. Eighteen. All marooned and left for dead in this blasted wasteland—an endless stretch of rust and haze. The Dethers said we ended up on the wrong side of the war, that it was a Turan's duty to die for their country.

I can't help thinking we have a different idea of duty. To die for one's country—sure, that's an honor for a soldier. But to be forced to fight until one went mad? To test the limits of their sanity? That's a different story.

The war started months ago, but it's been three weeks out here.

Now only one of us remains. It didn't matter how hard I tried urging the others on; they eventually stopped moving. I didn't.

My feet trudge through the ankle-deep sand, my legs stiff and tough as iron. I need to keep in motion, to ease the burden pressing on my chest.

As if the desert seeks to complicate the endeavor, something flashes in the corner of my eye. A shadow.

Perhaps I've already gone mad.

But when I look behind me, I sigh in relief. It's just a bird. A roadrunner. And she's stalking me like one would its prey.

She doesn't even flinch when she notices my gaze has landed on her, and it's then that I realize why. One of her wings rests at an odd angle, and she's limping. She's desperately clinging to my shadow like I am to my water flask, trying to survive.

"How long have you been following me, girl?" I ask. Though roadrunners are bred for desert life, most of them reside in the grasslands, or at least, stretches of desert with lots more shade than this. She must be lost. And barely survived some sort of attack by the looks of it.

Suddenly, I feel a kinship with this bird. Two weary and battered souls, far from home.

Too far. The truth lies heavy in my chest.

My wife never wanted me to join the war effort in the first place. She had wanted me to stay with her.

"Turan will hold," she said. *"Our borders are strong."*

But a country's walls are only strong so long as the enemy doesn't prove greater. And Detherland was mighty. In Turan, access to the sea means power. The Dethers rely on us for imports, for travel, for…much. In their greed, their army waged war on our smaller country, taking most of my unit down in their bloodlust.

We were cast away into the recesses of Detherland's fiercest desert with nothing but a small flask of water strapped around our shoulders and naught but our underthings to keep us "cool."

"It's my duty to serve, Mira. I can't stand by and watch Turan fall."

But fall it did. We all did.

"You will come back, Nicoli. For me?" She eyed the sword hanging about my waist before placing her hand on my chest, her small stature barely meeting the underside of my chin.

"I will always come back for you, Mira. Always."

"Even this time. You promise?"

I hesitated for only a moment. Even now, I don't know why. *"I promise."* I pulled her into an embrace. I felt her tears sodden the front of my gray fatigues before I tucked a lock of auburn hair behind her ear and backed away. I left her with a parting kiss. A kiss I can still feel if I trace my fingers over my lips.

Mira.

But now, trudging through this desert, I feel the weight of that empty promise and miss the weight of the sword at my hip. My gut heaves at the thought of the Dethers taking over Turan. Of them looting our homes and stealing our wives.

I drop to my knees and retch into a nearby stretch of cacti. But nothing comes out. No food for days and overly-rationed water deprive this sickness of its duty.

The roadrunner pauses, too, eyeing me in silent understanding. She isn't afraid, merely curious in my shadow, as if relying on my spirits—what little there may be—to bolster her own.

What a sorry lot we make.

I force myself to stand and press onward, my knees shaking violently. I must keep moving. I need to find my way home.

Every second that ticks by is a reminder of the fragility of life. How can a drop of water sustain so much and yet the lack of it turns the world to dust? I have enough to hold me over for at least two days more, the rationed drops another reminder of how my comrades had failed.

I need to keep moving.

"I love you," Mira called to my back as I headed out the door.

Her words bolster *my* spirit. Her love is the only thing that sustains these wearied limbs now.

"I love you more," I called back to her.

And it's true. I know of nothing that can challenge the love I have for my wife. Not even the heat of this cursed wasteland.

I plod onward, beads of sweat casting rivulets across my hairline and down my cheeks. I don't bother wiping them.

Step after step, I nearly stumble as my knees buckle. I catch myself as the roadrunner dances around my ankles and bring my gaze once more to the wavering horizon. I gasp.

A familiar woman in white stands in the distance. Her auburn hair almost matches the landscape. Her eyes look haunted, and before I can take a step forward, she collapses onto the sand with a cry.

Mira? "Mira?" I yell.

Can it be? In this godforsaken place?

I run to her limp form, my steps emboldened by my need to

touch her. Hold her. Look into her eyes.

I crouch in front of my wife and scoop her into my arms. The breath hitches in my throat; she's even more ethereal than I remember. And strangely light, too, as if she lacks substance.

A sprig of anticipation, or something like hope, winds its way through my chest. Mira has come to find me. She's gotten away from the Dethers. She's safe.

Her pale eyelids flutter open, and she stares up at me. "Nicoli?" she whispers.

"Yes, my love. I'm here. I promised we'd see each other again, remember?" My heart pounds blood to my ears.

"You didn't come back." Her eyes widen, and she reaches a soft hand to my cheek. Her touch is light like a feather, as if she herself were the roadrunner lost in the desert, like a breath of wind caressing my skin. "You...you left me. All alone."

Her words are like a slap. Oh, how I wish more than anything I could have evaded the Dethers and kept her safe myself. But the past is littered with follies and if-onlys. All we have is now. And the future.

"I was on my way. I only had a few miles more to go." My argument sounds weak, even to me. But it's the truth. I would traverse desert after desert in order to get back to her. But now I don't have to.

My wife suddenly coughs, the motion racking her body in violent bursts. "So thirsty…water..."

My hands go to the flask around my neck, and I hesitate a moment. These few drops will only last two more days. It's not enough for the both of us. But my wife, my love—her life is more precious than mine.

I uncork the top of the bottle and bring the edge to her mouth. Tipping the rejuvenating liquid in, I watch in horror as it evades her lips, feeling the cool splatter of it hit my knee instead.

The roadrunner comes out from my shadow and begins drinking the liquid frantically as if she hasn't tasted any in weeks.

I try shooing the bird away and focusing my attention back on my wife. "You must drink, love."

I tip the flask once more, and the same dreadful thing happens. My knee continues getting wet, her throat is still parched, and the roadrunner slurps up the water instead.

"Water…" she rasps.

I empty out the remaining contents of my flask and hope it's enough. Droplets dot her cheeks, but it's still my knee which has received most of the liquid and, subsequently, the roadrunner's stomach.

I pull her closer. I tug her nearer, but in doing so, I feel as if I'm embracing a corpse. As if I'm only caressing a shadow. A mirage.

Something isn't right.

Suddenly, my throat constricts, begging for relief. I've forgotten the taste of water on my tongue and the cool feeling of it running down my throat. With shaky hands, I lift the flask to my lips.

But nothing comes out.

Desperate, I bend over and lick the remaining water off my skin, but it's of little use. The roadrunner has already drunk most of it, and I taste only salt. Nothing can quench this growing thirst.

I fall to my side, grasping my arms around my middle, and

breathe in the dust.

I feel so dry. So empty.

"Mira?" I rasp, barely audible even to myself.

I try to stand, but my fatigued limbs revolt against the effort. My heart nearly trips with a sudden realization: I've stopped moving. I've succumbed to the fate of my comrades.

"Mira?" I call again, louder, clawing at the grains of sand.

Where is she? Where is my love?

"Water, Mira." My body heaves in desperation and suddenly stills, waiting…

I know she'll come back for me. She has to. Our love is stronger than these parched sands. Maybe she'll even bring me something to quench this insatiable thirst. Maybe it will be enough to keep me going.

And find my way home.

To feel her kiss once again.

Mira.

***

When I open my eyes, I expect to see whiteness, like how dying is described in all the books I've read back home.

But instead, I see a waning sun, dipping below the horizon. A coolness replaces the blazing heat, and it's then that I acknowledge my state. I'm covered in sand with dust particles caked in the corners of my eyes. I can hardly open my mouth without needing to cough from the dryness, and my lips are chapped to the point that dried blood rests in the cracks.

But I'm alive.

I lift my head a fraction and see the roadrunner sitting beside me, her broken wing lying awkwardly by her side and her head folded into her breast. Resting.

She stayed.

Maybe she thinks I have more water to dole out. The memory of the bird stealing it all comes back in a flash. But if not the bird, then it would have been the sun or the sand. Better someone's thirst was quenched than no one's at all.

Regardless, she's still here. And for some reason, her presence brings comfort. After losing Mira all over again in a fleeting apparition, companionship is most welcome. So I don't have to grieve alone.

I shift my position, feeling the aching in every limb, and the bird opens her eyes, watching me. She stands up, ruffling her feathers before drawing nearer and poking me with her beak.

She looks at me as if assessing my health. Eager to know if I can stand.

"I'll manage," I somehow croak.

How can I carry on without water? Water is life in the desert. And I wasted all my remaining drink on fulfilling an empty promise.

Mira. But I'd do it again in a heartbeat if it meant keeping her alive.

There must be a reason why I'm still breathing. There's purpose in the parched places, right? I've been told beauty can be made from ashes, but what if I'm the ashes and there's nothing *good* to be found here at all? Why hasn't this barren wasteland burned up the last remnants of who I once was? Of who I am now?

The roadrunner coo-coos next to me, distracting me from my spiraling thoughts. Her dark comb sticks straight up, and when she turns her head, a single eye bores into mine.

Maybe the answer is many things.

One of them being the hope of seeing my wife—the *real* Mira—again.

And the other being laced with feathers.

When I was left here to die, the small bird had found me and latched on as if her very life depended on mine.

She's injured, and I can tell she needs my help every time she looks at me. It's as if she's relying on me to bring her somewhere. To rescue her. I may have lost my Mira, but maybe all is not fully lost if I can give of myself one last time. To this poor creature with everything to lose and nothing to gain.

If my only reason for taking a few more steps is because of an injured bird, so be it.

I won't let this roadrunner waste away.

I groan as I bend my knees, preparing to get up. Black dots cloud my vision when I push upward, but I blink a few times and shrug it off. Dizziness should be expected.

There's nothing left for me to do but walk or else succumb to death.

I can't recall the minutes, maybe hours, of travel, but every step becomes easier than the last under the cover of moonlight. My body aches, and my chest hurts from the haunting memory of my wife, but still I press on.

The roadrunner coo-coos by my feet, struggling to maintain my stride, and it's then that I bend down to pick her up. "If you don't mind, we can cover more ground this way." She doesn't protest, just nestles in the crook of my elbow as if she's been waiting for this moment to rely on my strength to carry her to safety.

Where am I even going? With no roadmap, this feels like an endless pursuit. Where is Turan in the midst of the Detherland desert? Which direction do I turn to?

"You will come back, Nicoli. For me?"

"I will always come back for you, Mira. Always."

"Even this time. You promise?"

Our conversation from a few months ago echoes in my head. I don't know how much longer I can carry on without a drop of water. But I must have been walking for a long time because suddenly the beginnings of a sunrise form along the horizon.

Urgency courses through my bloodstream. Once that sun crests the sand dunes, I'll be cooked. In more ways than one. And the roadrunner will be no better off than she was before.

"Just a little more," I say, trying to assure the bird, though I know she doesn't understand me. *More empty promises.* "We'll get help soon."

I press on, telling myself to keep placing one foot before the other. But with each step, I feel the heat increase. The rate in which the sun climbs the sky is alarming, and I'm already preparing myself for the inevitable.

I'm so sorry, Mira. Maybe death will come swiftly.

Something bright flits by my head and lands on a nearby cactus. A kingfisher calls into the morning, welcoming the new day. And another some distance away answers.

And then a hare darts across my path, nearly getting caught

between my legs. I could have sworn I saw another one a few miles away.

And then I spot oleander in patches, dotting the once-barren landscape. And the further I walk, the purple plant only continues to spread.

These plants. Animals. That must mean... "Water," I cry, my knees almost giving way when I spot a small oasis in the distance.

Clutching the bird to my chest, I walk-sprint as fast as my body will allow. And once at the stream, I'm grabbing palmfuls of water and shoveling the liquid into my mouth. The roadrunner gulps the water beside me, her gentle cooing a sign of her delight.

Water has never tasted so sweet.

When I glance up, my heart leaps to my throat at the pair of boots standing in front of me. I follow those boots upward and find to whom they belong: an old man, a Detherland native by the looks of it.

And behind him, I spot a distant village nestled in a desert valley, the landscape slowly changing from orange to green. Relief pools in my middle. *We've made it out alive.*

"You look like you've been to war," the man says, cracking a toothy smile.

I swallow another handful of water before answering. "I have."

His smile drops. "The war between Turan and Detherland?"

I nod.

"That was over two weeks ago. You've been out here this whole time?"

I nod again. *Wait.* "The war's ended?" Is it too much to hope?

Now it's his turn to nod. "Detherland has claimed Turan for its own; we're one people now, the Greater Detherland. Prisoners have been returned home, too. You"—he looks at me askance—"and your bird are no longer exiles."

Home. The one word ignites something fiery inside me. Home means hope. Home means Mira.

I reach up and pull the man down by his collar. "Tell me. What did they do with the women and children? Where are my people? The civilians of Turan?"

I'm sure I look as crazed as I feel. But being stranded in the desert will do that to a person.

"Easy, son." He loosens my grasp and straightens. "As I recall, all women and children have been left alone. As a man of peace, that's my hope at least. Not all Dethers are bad. Both sides have fought hard for what they believe is right. Both sides have also been wrong."

I swallow hard. This isn't the answer I was hoping for.

"It might be worth going home," he says, that word stirring up longing once more inside my chest. "Much has changed, but enough has settled down now that resuming life shouldn't be too difficult."

Resuming life...not too difficult? Has he any idea of the hell I went through? I spent every night thinking about my Mira, hoping—praying—she still lived. And now, life was to be resumed like the war had never happened except for the Greater Detherland!

By this time, the roadrunner has cozied up next to me, practically begging to return to my arms. I oblige and lift her to my chest once more. Her small frame cools the rising anger inside me enough for clarity to come through. Shame fills me instead.

No. This man isn't to blame. He's not the soldier who sent me into exile. He's not the one who sent me away in the first place. He's innocent of the crimes pitted against me and my fellow comrades buried in the desert, each of their graves marked with whatever I could find.

I swallow my pride and meet his gaze. "Where…" I pause, still trying to find my tongue. "Which direction does old Turan lie?" I haven't been here before; I have no idea where I am.

The man smiles, pointing down into the valley. "A two days' journey through desert country and old Detherland. You'll find your home there, I hope."

I hope so, too.

I refill my canteen and guzzle another handful of water before standing. Already I feel strength returning to my bones. I make ready to cross the stream and head in the direction the man pointed when his hand on my shoulder stops me.

"You're famished. Here, take this." The man reaches into his pocket and offers me a wrapped parcel. I don't question his mercy as my fingers tremble opening it up. Inside is a half-bitten bread roll, but to me it's a delicacy.

It's devoured before I can even comprehend its flavor, the roadrunner nestled in my arms gobbling up her piece of the offering. The pair we make: two hungry souls once lost but finding hope in bread crumbs.

"The bird, son." The man interrupts the feast. "You'll take her from her home?"

I turn my gaze from the now-empty parcel to the small creature staring back at me. It's true we haven't been acquainted for long, but without her, I wouldn't have found the strength to keep going. I wouldn't have even gotten back up to stand.

I run my thumb over the roadrunner's forehead and listen to her gentle coo-coos in response. I can tell she's content—safe—and there's no way I'm leaving her behind. "I *am* her home," I say and then continue my journey.

With each step I take, I replay the same conversation over and over again in my head.

"You will come back, Nicoli."

"I will always come back for you, Mira."

My strides become longer, and I feel my strength returning.

"For me?" she asks again.

"Always."

My response is always the same.

"Even this time. You promise?"

With the roadrunner tucked between my arms and a lightness in my heart that wasn't there before, I smile. Genuinely, for the first time in months. Even though much has changed, I'm going home. *Home.*

"Yes. Even this time."

The End

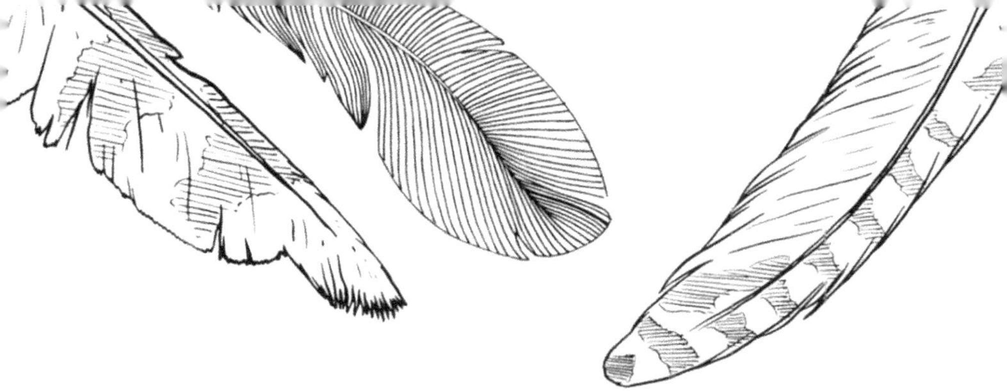

Whimsy

(poetry & quotes)

Hope for a Marigold

Marigold looked outside at the falling snow,
the last touches of autumn buried beneath
mounds of crisp white.
  "Will the flowers be cold?" she asked aloud,
but the noisy Blue Jay's squawk was her only reply.
So she sat and stared until warm tears
ran down her cheeks, chilling her skin
so near the frosted panes.
  "Goldie, my dear, what troubles you so?"
A woman in a white muslin gown sat beside her.
  "Oh, Mamma, I fear they'll die and be gone forever,"
Marigold said amidst sobs, her little finger on the window,
pointing to the ground.
A gentle hand stroked her cheek, drying the tears.
  "My child, why fear the snow when, in a few short months,
  the flowers will come again? They don't fear the cold.
  In fact, they are only sleeping,"
  "Sleeping?" Marigold looked more closely.
  "Why yes, and only beneath a blanket of snow. And when
  the blanket lifts, it will reveal a set of new buds, ready
  to bloom. But rush them not, for their time has not yet come."
And with that, her mother planted a gentle kiss on her brow
before walking away, her parting words still lingering.
  But rush them not, for their time has not yet come.
Marigold looked outside once more—smiling—filled with
new anticipation at what beautiful colors awaited the earth
beneath a blanket of white.

Amongst the Leaves

When the leaves fall,
do they realize it's to their doom?
That by loosening their hold,
it means their end?
They linger precariously,
like fledglings at the edge
of a nest, testing their weight
and letting the wind
rustle their feathers.
And the both of them fall—
if lucky, the one soars
in the sky while the other
cascades along a lazy river of
wind, only to find itself
upon the trodden earth.
The bird flies freely,
and the leaf falls to its end.
But is it truly the end?
Can beauty exist amongst death?
Are seasons only the markers of
loss, reminding us of
what once was?
But wait.
Listen…
Do you hear that?
The sound of heavy footsteps,
a little girl's bright laughter,
a family of deer nestling—
it's all amongst the leaves.
The crunching and rustling,
the breaking and shifting,

the giggles and joy—
it's all amongst the leaves.
The small child bursts forth
from the trees, tossing balls of
fiery oranges, reds, and yellows
in the air while her father
shifts them with his boots,
forming pictures along the ground.
And a family of deer watch,
hiding themselves amongst the
colorful foliage.
And I think:
This is beautiful. That perhaps it's
possible that beauty does indeed
exist amongst decay.
The thought warms my middle.
Two dissimilar things
occurring in tandem.
Seasons often are dichotomous,
mixing both beauty and grief.
And though it may bring discomfort,
it is not the end.
There is hope, even as the
leaves fade and die.
There is always hope.

A Path in Autumn

A path in autumn
Highlighted by marks of reds
And greens.
A golden ray of light
Leaving curious shadows
Filtering through the trees.
A cheerful titmouse
Flitting, soaring, and dancing
Alongside the bees.
A chipmunk with its friends
Tumbling and rolling as they
Run with ease.
What compares to sights
Such as these?
It all happens along
A path in autumn.

Stories

There are stories that take us places, whisking us away to far-off realms.
Stories that assuage the hurt spaces in our hearts and others that crack and bruise it.
There are stories that tell us who we are and others that make us lose ourselves along the way.
And then there are stories that feel like coming home, as if they've been part of us all along.

The Twig

Touching pen to paper is only the beginning. With each curl of ink, letters form and words begin turning into living, breathing things.

A landscape with mountains bursting through the sky and trees dotting a hillside, a heavy wind and a snapping of twigs until one finds itself floating along a lazy river and into the adjoining ocean, a mass that stretches for miles and glistens in the evening sunlight.

Months go by and the twig presses on, riding wave after wave until its frame hits the side of something much larger than itself: a ship swaying in the midst of the Blue, rocking to the tune of the sea.

Gulls and barn swallows circle the vessel, seeking a place to land. One gull swoops low and picks up the stick.

And there's music. Fiddles, lutes, voices. Songs dance on the wind from the crew below, the waves crashing against the ship's hull, adding bass to the merry cadence.

The captain suddenly emerges from his quarters, coattails billowing behind him, and the music ceases. His weariness speaks volumes: he'd rather the merriment die if all that's left for his crew is the approaching war. They're to go to battle within a fortnight.

One of the crewmen hands him a bodhran, encouraging him to cling to the hope the music brings. But the mallet is missing.

The gull, realizing the fish is simply a twig, drops the offending piece of wood. It falls through the sky only to land on the captain's head, tumbling to the deck like an offering.

The captain bends to pick it up, assessing its weight in his hand. It's strong and sturdy, tried and tested as if it's seen much of life and survived.

With one look at the crew, their heads nodding, he finds courage to strike one note.

And then another.

For the twig had come to him when his need was greatest. Maybe hope wouldn't be such a bad antidote for his grief.

With each tap on the drum, he finds his weariness comforted, though not fully sated. For death is cruel, but maybe hope resounds the greater.

For it comes like a gift. Like a twig traveling from the land to the sea.

And it's never lost.

Gift of Light

Be thankful for the hard things.
By them, we're able to
gauge the good.
For without darkness,
how would we appreciate
the gift of light?

Grace

A flower isn't planted and
expected to bloom in that
same moment.
Nor is a tree ready to give
wanderers shade when it's
merely a sapling.
Growth requires time, and
each season is due its grace.

Foothills

Most people climb mountains
for the views,
and a journey up one
takes perseverance.
With each new step,
though you get closer to the top,
it gets harder.
The temperature drops,
the wind picks up speed.
Pretty soon you're in a cyclone,
a wind tunnel, a gale.
But the views—they make the arduous
trek worth every ounce of struggle.
The views—they are breathtaking,
perched up high like a bird
surveying its land.
You almost think it's
possible to fly.
But at a mountain's base,
one feels small and insignificant,
reminded of the minuscule quality of humankind.
Glancing upward at the tall rocks gives glimpses
that there's Someone far greater—
Mightier—than ourselves.

Most people climb mountains
for the views—
and as breathtaking as they are
I go to them for the foothills.

Bursting

There are moments
When I come close
To bursting—
As if my heart
Has sprouted wings,
Beating against my
Rib cage
To break free from
Its fleshy prison.

It beats not from
Panic or fear—rather
From a yearning,
A longing,
A desire,
To embark on a quest,
To discover new lands
And watch as the
Painted landscapes
Fill my mouth with song—
A melody sweet and
Savory, recalling stories
Amongst the wind
And mountains.

The Mockingbird's call
Mimics a cry of my own
As it soars through the clouds
And whistles the tales
Of weary travelers and
Valiant men and women

Who once trekked these
Foothills and stood
Where I stand now.

A serpentine wraith
Slithers along the dusty
Crust of earth, its tongue
Licking the clay.
There are stories in its
Movements, memories
And dark deeds
Which it can no
Longer outrun.
I watch as its diamond
Back escapes into
          The brush.

And there are hares,
Bounding on their
Hind feet, retreating to
The shadows and
Leaving nothing but
Dust clouds behind them.
They guard their homes
Carefully, warding off
Predators through
Skillful evasion.
Their cottontails remind
     Me of the retreating clouds,
     The sky telling stories of
     Its own.

Peering through the trees,
Like curtains by a window—

The world unfurls in
Brilliant blues and oranges,
Greens and golds.
The trees sway with
The wind, and the
Rocks tremble with
The vibrations of
            The earth.

These are the kinds of
Things that inspire me,
The kinds of things
Which set
My soul to
            Bursting.

Castles

Towers built of stone
are more than mere houses.
They are memory keepers
of ages past
whose corridors
whisper secrets of their own.
In them you'll find
the adventure you seek,
but also a history so rich,
a remnant of kings, a
story as old as the timeless tales.
And if you listen long enough,
perhaps you'll hear the
faeries whispering amongst
the trees to the sparrows,
telling you their stories, too,
a history long since past
and forgotten by many.
And perhaps,
by their words,
you linger longer still.

A Fluttering of Feathers

There are moments where being
In love feels like flying,
Soaring high above tree tops
And chasing the sun—
Other times it's found in the
Mundane, the routines,
The ebbs and the flows of
All that it means to be human,
More of an existence
Rather than a fluttering of feathers.
But most often, it's
A hand to hold or squeeze,
A face to kiss goodnight
And good morning as
The sun sets and rises,
Knowing that no matter how
Or what or why,
They are always there
To stay.

Sunsets and Silhouettes

Three weary travelers
eager to get to their destination
and frustrated by the
lengthening shadows, throw
their voices to the sky.
"More, more!" the first begs.
"This confounded sun,
why must you set so soon?"
the second pleads.
"Why do your hours pass
like the coming rain,
lingering for only a breath?"
the third complains.
And the answer is met
with profound silence.
A silhouette of a tree extends
a branch toward the sky
where a rook, with leafy twig
in hand, paints the expanse
a pallet of orange, red, and blue.
Then comes a whisper—
whether from the bird or the tree,
or possibly both at once:
"Have you no care? Time is
not yours to control. Hastiness
doesn't equal success.
Slow, slow, and lean into the sun
For time is best when given,
not won."
The weary travelers look up,
catching a glimpse of the sky.

And instead of complaining and
continuing on their journey,
they pause.

Currents

There's nothing like writing and music.
One paints the scene, grounding you in something solid,
while the other allows you to soar amongst the clouds, riding the
currents of melodies.
I often find you can't have one without the other.

My Favorite Birds

When it comes to birds,
I'd be remiss
If I didn't tell you my favorites
In one succinct list.
It starts with the Tufted
A Titmouse of spring
With a comb of gray
And peach under wings.
And then there's the Flicker
A Northernmost queen
With the yellowest feathers
That you've ever seen.
Don't forget the Bluebird
An Eastern one, too
Whose cobalt and orange
Is sure to woo you.
And the striking-red Cardinal
Of Northern delight
Who feeds his beloved
And mates her for life.
The Gray Catbird is next
And yes, what a name.
It cries like a cat;
They're one in the same.
Behold the Barred Owl,
Known for its call
"Whooo cooks for you
Whooo cooks for you all?"
There are plenty more birds
Some big and some small
But I'll end it right here
For I can't list them all.

Little Magic

Sunshine on dewy grass. A cool breeze on a warm
day. A catbird's song after a storm. Bare toes
tingling before jumping from a cliff into a lake. Snail mail at
the perfect time. The double takes in the mirror
before the first date. Long-time lovers holding
hands, wrinkled with age.

The little things in life are their own kind of magic.

Cat

Your days are filled with
Lounging and eating.
You wake up just to stretch;
You eat just to sleep yet
Again. And I keep
Wondering if you're missing
Out on the beauties of the
Waking world—
Like the bird in the sky
Or the fox in its den…
But then I pause,
Perhaps you've got
It all figured out.
What's life without
A million dreams?

Aliferous

My wings are arms
My talons are feet
Oh to have a tail
Wouldn't that be neat?
My beak's a pair of lips
My feathers are skin
Alas, I'm no bird
To my chagrin.
But I've got a mind,
And I know it is thus
That in my heart
I'm still aliferous.

Nature Dances

It's considerate,
really,
of the wind
To engage
the leaves in a dance,
To howl and chirp at them
in song—
A raucous cacophony—
Reminding them
That life's too short
to just wait for
fall.

Barefoot Adventure

There is nothing so explicitly indicative
of adventure than bare feet and a cloak—
one to feel the wind currents between your toes
and one in which to ride them with wings.

Spring's Wonder

I awake to the smell of dirt and grass
Alerting me of the season's pass
From the chill of winter to the warmth of spring,
It's surprising what a new day will bring.
A clutch of blue in a robin's nest?
Or a strike of red on a grosbeak's chest?
The world is full of wonder anew
At the turn of each season or two.

Rain

Whenever the sky deems it fit to weep,
drenching the earth in its torrent,
my spirit lightens.
It's comforting to be understood
by the rain.

My gaze lifts toward the sky,
the droplets speckling my skin
with their cool touch.
"I love the rain," I say.

"Why?" my friend asks,
her raincoat a refuge against the storm.

I smile, staring at the dark clouds above
as they glide across the heavens in a
graceful dance like the grackles.
"Because during the times I've grown numb,
it's helped me to feel something. It reminds
me I'm not alone. That my unshed tears
have a space to belong
should they fall."

249

Skyward

If your eyes are on the ground, you'll miss the sunrise.
If your eyes are on the ground, you'll miss the eagle crest the treetops.
If your eyes are on the ground, you'll miss hope glimmering on the horizon,
    calling out with its resounding song:
    Hold on, hold on. And just look up.

Flight Patterns

What does it look like to
be as confident as
a sparrow,
to never question the
identity and
purpose it's
been given?

Goodness Looks Blue

Goodness hits a little different
when you're only expecting negative things.
In the midst of darkness, light feels
unfathomable, far off.
A wonder, a gift.
It's like an Eastern Bluebird descending
on a field of crows…
Its stunning beauty a beacon
of cobalt and peach amongst
squawking, writhing shadows.

Scattered Seeds

God has called the plants up
And He's called the soil to nourish.
He Who waters and gives life to all things,
Can grow life even from the pains of transition.
For He leaves no bird unfed
Nor flower overlooked and discarded
No matter how far the seeds scatter.

Even in the hard, He makes beauty bloom.

Land & Sea

Can you tell me the place where
the sky meets the earth—
Where the heavens kiss the sea
and the ships make berth?

Can you tell me the place where
the mountains reach the heights—
Where stars 'round the peaks
dance with ethereal lights?

Can you tell me the place where
green pastures meet spring—
Where poppies and bluebirds
grow petals and wings?

Can you tell me?

Birds Are Birds

I've always wanted to fly,
reaching heights across the sky.
To soar freely and safely on outstretched wings—
the kind only found on feathered things.
If I was a bird, then perhaps I might,
but with arms and no wings, I can't take flight.
But I can dream and birds cannot;
a fair gift I know that can't be bought.
For dreams are quite magical things,
where a girl like me can find her wings.
I have my thoughts and love of words,
but I'm still human and birds are birds.

The Art of Observation

Can you graze your fingers against the hazy dark of a night sky?
Catch a falling star?
Touch the silver lining of the moon?
We don't have to hold beautiful things in order to know their worth.
Just marveling is enough.

Marvelous Wings

A snake doesn't long to fly,
nor does a bird wish to be
a crawling beast
when it's been given
such marvelous wings.

Why, then, do we look to others
and want what they have
when we've been given much
by the Creator Who
makes all things?

Night Sounds

I love hearing owls call out in the night.
It gives life to what appears dead and dark,
Adding a touch of light amidst the shadows.
Who knew a sound could feel so much
Like a spark of hope?

Canvas Sky

There's an unassuming grace
In the first lights of dawn
That comes slowly and softly,
Cresting the treetops beyond.
The Artist takes out His paintbrush
And with each purposeful stroke,
Casts streams of colors among the clouds
In wafts of red and gold smoke.
The sky is an endless tapestry
Where wonders weave anew.
It's enough to lighten burdens,
Making them few.
If the Artist takes such care
Painting His canvas sky
Then how much more so He cares
For you and I.

Birdsong

For so long, I've been the bird
Singing an endless song,
Awakening the leaves
And trees to stirring.
Day after day after day
Until my song fell short
And I lost my voice
And there was naught
To do but listen.
So I sat in silence,
Gazing at the sky
And that's when I heard it—
A song sweeter than any
I'd ever learned to sing
On my own.
A song birthed from light itself—
More light than song—
Resounding all around me
And filling my soul to bursting.
I soaked it in and swayed
To its rhythms, accepting
The purity of the notes
Until I learned to sing again,
But this time, to the tune
Of my Maker.

Tree Stumps

I find I'm a lot like a
tree stump. Weathered,
stubborn, and hard. But
I'm not all bad, you see.
I'm now a table for the
woodland faeries, a
pedestal for the foxes,
and a seat for the weary
wanderers. Yes, I may
not be what I once was,
but I'm nonetheless
beautiful.

Always in Full Bloom

As I look to the One who made the
Expanse above me
The land I tread,
And the seas below,
I'm reminded that it's He who
Causes the larks to sing
And the flowers to grow.
When my eyes are on myself,
I can only see so far,
My hands can only hold so much,
And my heart lies heavy with
Shoulders weighed down
By a trodden world, marred
By suffering and sin.
So I wait for the seasons
To pass—to come and go—
That I might find a spark
Of hope to cling fast.
And then I remember.
"Look up, dear child."
And see the expanse above me,
The land I tread,
And the seas below.
The One who made these,
And the flowers, in turn,
Is Lord over all the seasons,
Is He not?
And truth reigns supreme,
Singing a new tune.
And I know, because of Him,
Hope is always
In full bloom.

Golden Hills

When the sun descends
beyond the lowest hills,
be not discouraged.
The night is but a deep breath,
a gust of wind beneath an eagle's wings.
Come the dawn,
the sky will awaken
and paint those hills
in gold.

Endings
&
Things

Bird Glossary

American Crow (*Storm-Crow*) – large Corvus; all-black plumage; part-time scavenger; intelligent

American Robin (*Second Chance Robin*) – large migratory thrush; songbird; orange breast, worm-digger & appears at winter's end

Bald Eagle (*Skyward*) – large bird of prey; America's symbol of freedom; known for its white-feathered head

Barn Owl (*Crescent*) – medium-sized bird of prey; white-faced; nocturnal & silent in flight

Barn Swallow (*Stories in the Dark*) – medium-sized swallow; blue on top & peach below; long, deeply forked tail; symbolizes coming back home

Barred Owl (*My Favorite Birds; Crescent*) – large bird of prey; brown and white-striped plumage; silent in flight

Blue Jay (*Hope for a Marigold*) – medium-sized Corvus; blue and white plumage; loud, obnoxious call; intelligent

Buff Orpington Chicken (*Anna Belle and the Seed*) – buff/tan in color; most iconic chicken breed

Chipping Sparrow (*Flight Patterns*) – small songbird; red cap, striped wings & white belly; known for "chipping" call

Common Grackle (*Rain*) – large icterid; long-billed with blue-black iridescent plumage

Common Gull (*The Legend of the Lighthouse Keeper*) – medium-large seabird; web-footed; gray & white plumage

Common Kingfisher (*Parched Sands*) – small kingfisher; cobalt & peach plumage; long-billed; lives near water

Eastern Bluebird (*My Favorite Birds; Goodness Looks Blue*) – small, migratory thrush; cobalt on top & peach below

Eastern Meadowlark (*Always in Full Bloom*) – medium-sized blackbird; brown and black speckled on top & yellow and black plumage below

Eastern Screech Owl (*Crescent*) – small bird of prey; either gray or reddish-brown plumage; camouflage masters; tree dwellers & silent in flight

Eurasian Magpie (*The Swan and the Masquerade*) – large Corvus; black bodies with white patches; blue-green glossy wings

European Starling (*Coal of Smith-Harrow*) – medium-sized passerine; songbird; dark & glossy coat with white spots

Golden Eagle (*Like Stars in the Sky*) – large bird of prey; very fast; golden plumage

Gray Catbird (*My Favorite Birds; Little Magic*) – medium-sized songbird; all gray with russet tail; part of the mimic family & copies many sounds; known for "mewing" catlike call

Greater Roadrunner (*Parched Sands*) – long-legged & long-tailed cuckoo; mottled brown & tan plumage; lives in harsh climates

Green Barbet (*Storm-Crow*) – a tropical green bird; small-medium in size

Herring Gull (*The Twig*) – the most familiar of the gulls; gray & white plumage; beefy in size & shape

Leghorn Chicken (*Anna Belle and the Seed*) – known for their white bodies & red combs; hearty egg layers

Mute Swan (*The Swan and the Masquerade*) – large swan of the waterfowl species; white with black face and orange bill

Northern Cardinal (*My Favorite Birds*) – large songbird; male is a bright red & female is a muted brownish red; thick bill & long tail; sweet bird call

Northern Flicker (*My Favorite Birds*) – large woodpecker; black scalloped plumage; a ground feeder; bright yellow underwings in the east; bright red underwings in the west

Northern Mockingbird (*Bursting*) – medium sized songbird; gray plumage with striking white underwing markings; endless singer

Peregrine Falcon (*Captain Maverick of Tarkin*) – large, crow-sized bird of prey; dark, blue-gray plumage above & white below

Red-tailed Hawk (*The Tale of Markhus Roder*) – large bird of prey; mottled-brown plumage & russet-red tail; rounded wings

Rock Pigeon (*Coal of Smith-Harrow*) – also known as the rock dove; tubby & short; bluish gray plumage with black bands near tail

Rook (*Sunsets and Silhouettes*) – large Corvus; glossy blue-black plumage with a white face

Rose-breasted Grosbeak (*Spring's Wonder*) – large bird in cardinal
family; seed-eating; black plumage above & white below
with rose-colored throat

Snowy Owl (*Crescent*) – large bird of prey; all-white plumage
with brown scalloped markings on wings; silent in flight

Tawny Owl (*Crescent*) – medium-sized bird of prey; brown
plumage with mottled streaks; territorial & nests in trees;
silent in flight

Tufted Titmouse (*My Favorite Birds; A Path in Autumn*) – small
songbird in chickadee family; gray above & rust
underwings; known for its gray mohawk

White Stork (*Like Stars in the Sky*) – large wading bird; white
plumage with black wings; long, stilt-like legs

Wyandotte Chicken (*Anna Belle and the Seed*) – comes in 9
varieties; typically, a brown egg-layer

Ways to find out more about these birds and other species:

- *Google the Cornell Lab of Ornithology or download
  the app (for birds in North America)*
- *Google eBird or download the app (for birds outside of
  North America)*
- *Google Cornell Lab Bird Cams to live stream various
  species*
- *Download the Merlin Bird ID app for sound
  identification*
- *Purchase a field guide of native birds around your
  area*
- *Visit a local bird sanctuary and feed the birds*

Acknowledgements

This part of writing a book is always one of my favorites; I love getting to thank all the amazing people who helped bring this story to publication. As you now know, this collection took *years* to write, and in a matter of a few months—thanks to so many of you—it's now out in the world.

I want to first begin by thanking my beta readers, Ella Meyer, Robin Degan, Sarah Baylor, and Morgan Giesbrecht, who read these stories before they went to my editor. You girls helped flesh out these characters and spurred my imagination to new heights! Thankful is an understatement.

To my editor and friend Micaiah Keough, who pored over this manuscript with such care and diligence. Thank you for always being so patient and thorough in your process, even when my past tense verbiage is borderline excessive. Working with you is always a joy!

To my proofreader and friend Caitlin Miller, who caught all those pesky little typos and really made these stories shine. Thank you for always being in my corner and encouraging me along the way. You're the best!

To my dear writing buddies Erin Phillips and Jordan Taylor Nilan, who spur me on in Christ's love, never cease to lift my spirits when I'm down, and celebrate every little victory with me. Kindred spirits, sisters, best friends… I am forever grateful for you both.

To my endorsers, Moriah Chavis, Anna Christine, Erica Dansereau, and Danielle Bullen. Thank you for taking the time to read *Aliferous* early, for encouraging me, and for being such wonderful supporters. So grateful for each of you!

A special shoutout to my friend Anna Christine. Thank you for making all the bird artwork that's included in the preorder goodies. May your brush always stroke and your creativity never run dry. Thankful for you!

Thank you to my family, as always, for being my cheering squad. Your encouragement and enthusiasm over each publication never gets old, and I'm forever grateful. Love you all!

A special thank you to my husband, Zac, and our floofy cat, Moo. You both have been my rocks these past seven years and now we get to add a little one (human, not animal) to the bunch next month. So amazed by the Lord's blessings.

And on that note, thank you to my Lord and Savior—Jesus Christ. You are the heart of these stories, the heart behind why I write, and the reason why I can take up my pen in the first place. Without you, there would be no *Aliferous*. You are the reason we hope, find our courage, and can spread wings of our own. Thank you, always.

And thank you, dear readers, for taking the time to pick up this collection and dive in. I hope it brought some comfort and encouragement.

Alissa J. Zavalianos grew up in New Hampshire and currently lives there with her wonderful husband and their adorable cat Moo. As a child, she always had a love for nature, books, and fairy tales, and as she grew older, that love bloomed all the more. Alissa loves Jesus and is inspired by birds, mountains, castles, Tolkien, Lewis, and the way a cold breath of wind feels on her bare toes.

Feel free to follow Alissa on her website https://alissazav.wixsite.com/website and on Instagram @authoralissajzavalianos.